The Mansion

Donna M. Bryan

DEDICATION

This book is dedicated to my children who have encouraged me to write down my stories. Special thanks to my daughter Brenda for all her help in getting this published.

I also want to acknowledge the wonderful assistance of those in my writer's group for their critiquing.

Thank you very much!

THE MANSION

Donna M. Bryan

CHAPTER ONE

JC turned the squad car onto Prairie Road. There had been a report that lights were seen tonight in the old Murphy mansion. Willard Murphy had died two years ago and the house was empty. Old John who had been caretaker of the property for the Murphy family would have been home and sound asleep hours ago. The attorney who managed the estate while trying to locate any living relatives had retained John.

Old Mr. Murphy had come from a family of money and worked hard amassing its worth even more. He had been a pillar of the town and well known for his charitable nature. His son, William Murphy didn't share the work ethic and as an angry young man disappeared after an accident. It was assumed he had died in the crash but the authorities never recovered the body. He didn't make an appearance at the funeral of either parent. Mr. Jensen, the legal representative was still trying to locate William or any other family members to carry out the instructions that were in the will.

JC turned into the U shaped driveway and stopped in front of the dark home. A veranda went around the entire first floor with wide steps leading to the double wooden doors. The second floor had a balcony but not the third floor. She thought that was rather ironic because in the days when the mansion was built, that was where they held the dances and one would think stepping out into some fresh air would be nice on a warm evening.

Letting the desk sergeant know she was checking out the place, she picked up the large flashlight and exited the car. Touching her holstered gun, she adjusted her eyes to the dark and surveyed the house and surroundings. *I'll check the doors and see if they are locked. Could just be that old John had left a light on when he left and it burned out.*

Her black rubber soled boots didn't make a sound as she slowly climbed the steps. She could see the outline of the porch swing and other furniture and plants. She heard a click and then a light came on around the corner of the porch along with the sound of paper. There was someone here and it wasn't John. He would have greeted her. Unsnapping her holster, she removed her revolver, her senses heightened as she moved closer to the rounded corner, her eyes sweeping the area. Bending lower, she completed the move, gun ready to fire if necessary.

Sitting in a recliner was a stranger holding a pipe in one hand and a bag of tobacco in the other. "No need for the gun, officer."

Ignoring his request, she sternly asked, "Who are you, what are you doing here and why didn't you speak up when you heard me drive up?"

"I'm Benjamin Murphy, grandson of the late Willard Murphy. I saw what looked like a police car and figured if I moved you might shoot thinking I was a criminal." He smiled at her, "Now will you put that gun away, it makes me nervous.

JC lowered the 9 millimeter. The lamp light illuminated the area and JC assessed the man calmly remaining in the chair with the pipe in one hand and a bag of tobacco on his lap. He did resemble pictures she had seen of Mr. Murphy when he was a young man.

"May I see some ID?" She requested. *Anyone could say they were a relative because Attorney Jensen had been sending out inquiries on kin of Mr. Murphy, so this could very well be an impostor.*

"May I stand up to get my wallet from my pocket? I assure you, I am not trespassing. I have been to Mr. Jensen's office today and legally have the keys to my grandfather's properties." Benjamin smiled.

JC nodded, "Slowly."

Turning to the side of the chair to get both feet on the floor, he slowly stood up, removed his wallet, and taking out his driver's license, handed it to her. "If you would step inside, I can show you papers that I was at Attorney Jensen's office today."

Shaking her head no, she spoke into the radio on her shoulder, "Dispatch, please put a call to Attorney Jensen's home. I'm at the Murphy mansion and there is a man here who claims to be the grandson of Willard. Please verify. Thanks." She returned his driver's license that had a New York address.

"May I finish filling my pipe or would it bother you?" Benjamin looked at her.

"Go ahead." She stepped back just in case he would throw it at her she still had no proof he was who he said he was.

She watched as he lightly tamped down the tobacco in the bowl of the pipe and picking up a wooded stick match from a box on the small round table, swiped it across the box and lit the pipe, making soft sucking sounds as he drew in the first few puffs. A sweet cherry smell filled the air.

Her dispatcher came on, "Mr. Jensen said the young man is legit, long lost grandson of Mr. Murphy. You're finished up there." It clicked off.

"Satisfied Officer..." Benjamin looked at her name badge, "Smith?"

"I still want to know why you were sitting here in the dark when you saw and heard my vehicle in the driveway you didn't immediately identify yourself." Her blue eyes watching him carefully knowing you can tell a lot about people by their facial and body movements.

"All I saw as I was absorbing the surroundings in the quiet of the evening was a car come up the drive that looked like a police car in the dark, and someone go to the front door. For all I knew, you could have been robbing the place. Granddad has a lot of antiques in there. So, I just sat here quietly waiting to see if I had to punch 911 into my cell phone or not." He took another puff on his pipe.

"We in the Freedomville Police department take our duty seriously." Sliding her gun back into the holster, she looked up at him, "Do you realize you could have been shot by not speaking up?"

"I'm sorry. Did you know my grandfather very well? I don't know anything about him except what I've seen on this short excursion into this huge place." His voice was slightly forlorn.

"Everyone in town knew and loved him. He seemed so alone in some ways after your grandmother died. He was an outstanding person and missed by us all." The last few words she spoke very quietly.

Her dispatcher came on, "JC, you need to check out Ernie's Bar, looks like ole Jake has had one too many and may need a ride home. It's a quiet night, okay with you on the ride?"

JC laughed, "Okay with me."

"Gotta go, duty calls. I hope you enjoy the town." She said to Benjamin as she turned to leave.

"Wait, do you know someone that could give me the history lesson on my family, the town, and this beautiful mansion?" Benjamin swept his arm around to encompass the surroundings.

Hesitating for just a moment JC said, "Yes I do, me."

"Are you the town historian?"

"No, my grandpa and Mr. Murphy were very good friends and I played here a lot as a child and it was like a second home most of my life." The words came out quietly.

"There is so much I need to know about all of this: Granddad, the mansion, my past. Dad never told me a thing, he was very angry with Granddad, and mom didn't know anything either. Strange." A sober expression was on his face.

That comment from him caused a lot of questions JC would like to ask, but there wasn't time. She turned to go, "Duty calls."

"Wait. Could I impose on you to go through the mansion and tell me how life was here, my grandparents?" He was hoping she would say yes.

She hesitated for a brief moment. *Something about him intrigues me.* "I'm off tomorrow; I'll give you a call in the morning, say around ten or so, if I don't get called in for some reason."

Reaching out his hand to shake hers, "Thanks, I really would appreciate a tour."

"Tomorrow then, I really have to go." Giving him a nod of her head, she quickly went down the steps to the police car.

Benjamin watched the vehicle until it was out of sight. He took a puff on the pipe, the cherry tobacco giving a nice smell in the air. Somehow, it was calming to him as he pondered the situation of being here. He had noticed a pipe stand in the study and assumed his grandfather also liked to smoke a pipe. His dad had never smoked.

His parents had died in a plane crash; he had no siblings and now his grandfather that he didn't know he had, passed away. Did he have any other relatives? He was the sole owner of the law firm his dad started and now this. He felt alone. Most of the women he met were more impressed by his wealth as an easy ride to a rich life. Taking a few weeks off right now to learn of his past was a good thing.

Smiling in the dark he thought, *maybe Officer Smith would be a refreshing touch of a small town historian. New York went at a fast pace and everyone was out for the all mighty buck.*

Picking up his cell phone from the small table, he went into the house. It was time to write in his journal, a daily ritual. Tomorrow he should have the phone hooked up and the internet. He needed to purchase a printer and fax machine too. Maybe Officer Smith could help him with that too. It would be more interesting than going alone.

Benjamin turned the lock on the massive door. *I wonder if locking up the house at night is necessary in this small town where everyone seems to know everybody's business.*

Turning around and looking up at the portrait of his grandfather, "Granddad, there is so much about you I need to know. Between Mr. Jensen and Officer Smith, maybe I will learn why dad never spoke about you." He saluted the large painting and went into the office.

Sitting down in the huge wooden chair, he opened his journal and quickly jotted down the day's events. Then he made a list of things he wanted to accomplish the next day.

Tapping his pen lightly against his chin, he smiled. He was glad officer Smith agreed to come over and assist him in understanding more about his past. He was impressed by her. She performed her duties as a police officer, yet when they discussed his Granddad and the mansion, her attitude and facial expression changed as though they were discussing her

Granddad and home. He noticed what a beautiful shade of blue her eyes were and when he shook her hand; the skin was soft and smooth, but firm.

Something about her got to him. He didn't want her to leave; he wanted to talk more, like there was some connection to her. He was use to women fawning over him, batting their eyes and shimming up to him, all so pretentious. She wasn't like that. In his line of work he sized people up pretty fast. He hoped she called in the morning. He wanted to see her again.

Opening the desk drawer, he put his journal in it and picked up the huge ring full of keys Mr. Jensen had given him and studied them for a moment. Tomorrow he would start unlocking things and see what mysteries the cupboards, desks, and safe would reveal. But for now, he was tired, and felt he could sleep with ease. The mansion for being so huge, felt comfortable. Putting the keys back, he took the one for the desk, relocked it, taking a final look around, shutting off the light, left the room.

CHAPTER TWO

After JC delivered the inebriated Jake to his scolding wife, she had to smile remembering how upset Jake's wife was when she brought the man home. She shook her head, about once a month Jake went on a toot and they repeated the same routine.

Jake's wife was like a human bandy rooster jumping up and down hollering at him. Jake just closed his eyes and said, "Yes, Dear" and let her pull him into the house.

His wife was a teetotaler and JC doubted if she allowed mouthwash or vanilla flavoring in the house because there was some alcohol in them. So once a month ole Jake met with some of the guys after work for a beer, and then another round until Jake was feeling no pain, and he got a ride home and she started ranting at him about going to hell when he died. JC figured Jake probably slept through most of the tirade.

As she completed her uneventful shift, JC had plenty of time to go over her exchange with Benjamin Murphy. Looking at him as a woman and not a cop, she thought he oozed confidence and masculinity. He was dressed in expensive clothes and seemed comfortable in them. She couldn't understand why she accepted the invitation to go through the mansion with him except, she wanted too.

Part of it had to be curiosity about the grandson of ole Mr. Murphy. Her granddad had been a friend of Willard and as Chief of Police had been in the home many times for community events. She had been in the home on special occasions and since granddad had been a fishing buddy of Willard too, he often took her along. Mrs. Murphy would spend time with her when granddad and Willard were talking about a local concern.

JC wondered what Benjamin would do with the mansion and all the other property that Mr. Murphy owned in the surrounding county. After his wife passed away Willard had retired and managed his commodities and other businesses from home.

Mr. Murphy had provided for Old John in his will plus many others who had been faithful employees of his. Many charities, the small local hospital and the three churches also received healthy checks. He had always been a benevolent person while he lived and many people upon his death received anonymous gifts in forms of college funds, a paid up mortgage and for one family, a cruise for the injured military man and his family.

There was just too much of a mystery here. Two years after Willard's death, now a supposedly grandson shows up. Um. Supposedly William's body had never been recovered and here was a grandson. She was going to keep an eye on him.

It was sad that the mansion had remained empty all this time, but the thought that it would be sold or used as a commercial building filled her with sorrow. This mansion would always be a home to her, filled with laughter and special occasions for the town.

Well, maybe her inquisitive nature would be satisfied in the morning. Now all she had to do was figure out what to wear. Would he only want a tour of the mansion, or would they be uncovering furniture and sifting through things? Or did he just want to talk about the man he had never met, a family he never knew?

She also wanted to talk with Mr. Jensen tomorrow before she went out to the mansion and see if he was comfortable with his interview with Benjamin. She had conducted an inquiry on Benjamin before she left work and there wasn't even a traffic ticket on him.

She stood with one hand on her hip and surveyed the closet. Jeans, a tee shirt, light jacket and tennis shoes would be her comfortable dress for tomorrow. It wasn't like this was a date and if they were digging around it could be rather dusty although the house had been cleaned every month. Still she doubted the attic or basement had much done to them.

Removing her badge, unbuckling her gun and holster, JC placed them and other items from her pocket on the dresser. Then she sat down and unlaced the uniform boots and took them off. *Ah, that felt good. They were light weight, but still they were leather boots.*

She finished undressing and washed up for the evening.

Setting the alarm for six-thirty a.m., JC said her prayers and was asleep the moment her head hit the pillow.

* * *

Music from the clock radio woke JC from a refreshing night's sleep. Taking a quick shower, she dressed, put her long blond hair into a ponytail, and went to her desk to give Mr. Jensen a call. He was always in the office early on Friday if he had a court date.

"Good morning, Mr. Jensen, JC here. I just have a few questions about Willard's grandson. Are you sure he is the right one?"

"Well, ninety nine percent sure, JC. I had a detective agency investigating him because Willard never gave up the thought that William was out there some place and had searched through the years. He had some leads, which I turned over to the agency. I don't have a DNA to prove Benjamin's identity, but I'm satisfied to the extent of turning over Willard's estate to him. Why do you ask?"

"Because Benjamin asked if I would come over and tell him more about his grandfather, the town, tour the mansion, even about his dad's relationship with his grandfather. Does he have a family in New York?" JC was curious why no one came with Benjamin.

"No, he hasn't been married either. He is a brilliant lawyer and keeps very busy on important cases. There was the usual dating, going to public openings and the like, but he has really kept his nose to the grind stone. And since his dad died and he is sole owner of the law firm, busier than ever. I have to go, JC, but rest assured he is legit."

"Thanks, Mr. Jensen. Bye." They both hung up.

She nibbled on the side of her lip. *The lawyer is ninety-nine percent sure. But what if he was wrong about Benjamin? People pull scams all the time. She loved the mansion, Willard and Elizabeth. She would rather see it go on like it has been, people working, donations given to the community than to a charlatan.*

JC glanced at the clock, time to give Benjamin a call. He answered on the third ring.

"Good Morning, Benjamin. I was wondering if you still wanted to get together today." JC didn't have to wait for an answer.

"Yes, of course, anytime that is good for you is fine with me. I was just going to start breakfast, would you care to join me?" He waited for her answer knowing he was being rather forward.

"Ah, do you know how to cook and what's on the menu?"

"Bacon and eggs and yes I know how to cook, well a few things and this in one of them." He laughed and let out his breath, glad that she was accepting his invitation.

JC laughed, "Well, just in case you burn anything, I'll bring some bagels and cream cheese. I'm starving, so see you in about five minutes."

"Great, see you soon." Benjamin replied and hung up the phone.

Putting her badge and gun in her leg holster, her cell phone in her pocket along with a small plastic holder that held her driver's license and credit card, she grabbed the keys to her Jeep, took the package of bagels and cream cheese from the refrigerator then locked and closed the door.

Stepping out to the porch, she took a deep breath of fresh air and smiled, *it's going to be a great day.*

CHAPTER THREE

JC entered the horseshoe driveway at the stroke of eight. For some reason, she didn't feel nervous about spending some time with a total stranger. This old mansion held so many nice memories for her and to share them with Benjamin would be enjoyable.

Having left the front door ajar, Benjamin heard the crunch of a vehicle tires and stepped out onto the front porch. He glanced at his watch. He liked a person to be on time. After all, in his business, time was money. Benjamin was anticipating an informative day explaining some of his heritage.

He smiled as JC looked up at him as she came around the Jeep. Gone was the uniform, the tightly wound blond hair in a bun, the officer on duty. In front of him was something unusual: a woman without makeup, no artificial eyelashes, and her hair pulled back in a simple ponytail, wearing jeans, a tee shirt and tennis shoes. He was used to people trying to impress him.

Stepping forward, he extended his hand, "Good morning, Officer Smith. Welcome to my home. I appreciate you giving up your day off to assist me in my quest to learn more about the mansion and my family."

JC shook his hand, "Good morning to you too, and everyone calls me JC, short for Janice Caroline." With a grin, she raised the bag with the bagels and cream cheese, "I'm starved, I hope you started breakfast."

He motioned for her to go ahead into the home, "As a matter of fact, I just put the bacon on a paper towel and have the omelet ready to put into the pan."

As they both walked back to the kitchen, she could see that the furniture was still covered. *Did that mean he wouldn't be here very long?* Entering the spacious kitchen, she observed the small round kitchen table set for two.

Sniffing the aroma, JC remarked, "Um, the coffee smells good and I haven't had any yet today. What can I do to help?"

"I have biscuits in the oven, courtesy of those prepackaged ones. Do you mind if we save the bagels for later?" Benjamin looked at her over his shoulder.

"No problem." As she walked past him, she could faintly smell the clean masculine soap he showered with. He didn't look bad in those slacks and polo shirt either.

"While you are putting those in the refrigerator, you can bring out the cream for the coffee and the oranges I've peeled and sectioned for us." Benjamin tested the pan to make sure the temperature was right to pour in the omelet mixture.

JC went to the sink and washed her hands, then picked up the package she had brought and put it in the refrigerator and retrieved the requested items and placed them on the table.

"I see you like vanilla coffee creamer too. It's my favorite. Your grandfather liked flavored creamer too. Otherwise he would add sugar and plain cream to his coffee and I mean the good old whipping cream like you can whip up and put on dessert or in hot chocolate." Making herself at home, she picked up the coffee carafe and filled both mugs, leaving plenty of room for a generous amount of cream.

Dividing the omelet in half onto both plates, Benjamin looked over at JC, "You seem quite familiar with the kitchen." He placed the empty pan back on the stove and held the chair for her.

Um, manners, just like Mr. Murphy. No problem, she liked that in a man. "I should be comfortable with this kitchen. Your grandmother and I spent a lot of time here, helping me with my school lessons or baking cookies." Placing the napkin on her lap she looked over at him. "Both of my parents were killed in a boating accident and I lived with my grandparents after that. My grandmother was handicapped, a victim of polio, so I use to go along with grandpa most of the time when I wasn't in school. Since your grandfather and mine were close friends, I was here a lot." She smiled over at him.

"Did you know my dad?" Benjamin had placed his fork down and looked intently at her.

"No. I can honestly say I don't even remember him. I was just a baby and only knew him by the pictures around here. Good omelet by the way and the bacon is perfect. Do you cook a lot?" JC spread a little jam on her biscuit.

"Just enough so I can get by, nothing fancy. I have so many business dinner meetings or we order in and Betty, who manages my personal things, will whip up something if I need a small buffet or I have it catered. How about you, do you like to cook?" He added creamer to his coffee and gave it a stir with the spoon.

Laughing she leaned back into her chair, "Just the basics. I'm afraid I've always been something of a tom boy. I know how to fish, fire a gun, change the oil in my Jeep if I need to, but please don't ask me to make anything fancier than a grilled cheese sandwich. Well, I do know how to bake a fish in the coals along with some sweet corn. I told you I spent a lot of time with my grandpa."

Benjamin picked up the coffee carafe and looked at her.

"Yes, please." She held up her mug. "Police officers have coffee in their veins you know and we need to replenish it often." She nodded a thank you as he filled her cup.

"What do you want to do first thing this morning, Benjamin? I'm off this weekend and except for going to church on Sunday, I'm free to assist you." JC took a drink of her coffee. *She also wanted to observe on her own if Benjamin showed any unusual behavior that would raise any red flags as to his legitimacy of being heir to the massive inheritance Mr. Murphy had left.*

"If you don't mind, I need to go into town and purchase a printer with a fax. I called to have the internet and phone turned on." He laughed. "They told me they don't work on weekends and there was a back log. I said if it is on by seven this morning, there is a hundred dollar bill for them besides whatever they normally charge. Then when they heard it was here and who I am...well just say, I tried the phone and computer this morning and both are working. I didn't realize my grandfather had that much clout from the grave. But I still need the printer/fax machine."

Putting her fork down on her plate, in a quiet voice, JC asked, "Do you do that often...use money to get special privileges?"

"No, but in my line of work, time is money and to lose a case or maybe have a man go to jail because I didn't have the small piece of evidence in time, then I have no qualms waving some money to get what I need. I will gladly pay anyone that has to go the extra mile to assist me. It is their choice, but as they say, 'money talks'."

She nodded. *She agreed with that reasoning.* "Okay, let's load the dishwasher and go into town. We have a small mall but the old main part of town has an office equipment business. They also carry paper, ink and do custom printing service. I would suggest there." JC was stacking the plates as she talked.

"That sounds fine to me. When we come back, I'd like to explore the house more. I asked John to have whoever does the monthly cleaning to come in and remove the furniture covering. That should be completed by the time we come back. John will also have her stock the refrigerator for me. I need to look at the list of names Mr. Jensen gave me so I know whom I'm dealing with. Evidently, they were all employees of grandfather and he treated them like family. I find that amazing in this day and age to find that type of help. Do you mind driving? I flew in and grandfather's vehicles are in the garage, but I have no idea where to go." He leaned against the counter. "And for the record, I will pay them extra for doing more since I am here." He wanted to make sure she knew he wasn't taking advantage of the help.

"I know all of them, like I told you, I was here a lot. They are all wonderful, trust worthy people. Now," she looked at her watch, "The stores should be open, do you have any other errands besides the office supplies?"

"No, I don't. After you, JC," Benjamin gestured with his arm toward the door.

* * *

They completed the shopping trip with both of them receiving many glances and JC knew that the phones would soon be busy. Who was that handsome man JC was driving around in her Jeep?

As they drove up to the property, they could see someone on the riding mower making laps across the vast lawn. At the house, John was supervising the weeding of the plants the surrounded the porch and around the huge oak trees that shaded the mansion.

Benjamin shook his head, "I'm frankly amazed how well kept the property is. Mr. Jensen did tell me that grandfather had set up a provision for maintenance of the property until I was located. In my discussion with John yesterday, he said he uses high school and college students during the summer and has the housekeeper and a few others that want part time work during the winter."

Giving him a side-glance, JC added, "Old John use to handle all the maintenance except when many hands were needed. There were huge flower and vegetable gardens too. Now at his age, for the most part he mainly does a great job of supervising. He loves this place as if it was his own. When his wife died, your grandfather had him move into the guest cottage out back." She parked the Jeep and shut off the motor.

Entering the house with their purchases, they found all the furniture covering removed and a note saying lunch was in the refrigerator.

JC and Benjamin set up the equipment and the machine began printing immediately. "I told you money talks." He sighed. "I really hate that you know. We should all be on a system where we can have days off at different times so business doesn't stop on Friday. How many times do people need to see a doctor and the office is closed and they have to go to the hospital and endure the higher cost of the Emergency Department and many don't have that type of money or the insurance won't cover it." He shook his head side to side. "I spend many weekends working on briefs that must be ready for court on Monday. A simple thing like getting a necessary copy from the courthouse has to been done during the week. When new evidence gets to me on a Friday night, court convenes Monday morning... well you get the picture."

"Now, what can you tell me about this room, grandfather's office? I don't really know what to call him. I look at his picture in the hall and feel like I know him and I never met him, my dad never talked about him. Isn't that strange?" He sat down on the big old wooden chair behind the desk and patted the arms of the chair as he spoke.

"This room was personal for him. He didn't as a rule conduct business here. He had an office in town, until your grandmother passed away. Then he got a little reclusive. He slowed down a lot, but when people were here, he usually visited with them in the small living room or the garden room. Only granddad and I visited in here with him. It was like I was his grandchild too. Even as an adult, I was treated like I was part of their family. I liked that. My dad was an only child and I spent a lot of time with friends, but they aren't family."

She leaned against the desk and pointed at a mounted fish on the wall above the fireplace. "I was with them when your grandfather caught that fish. Boy did that fish give him a struggle. He said any fish that fought that hard shouldn't be dinner but put up on the wall as a fighter, a winner." JC was silent for a moment lost in that memory.

Looking over at Benjamin, she ran her hand along the top of the desk. "This desk he had made special for him. There was a carpenter in town with a large family that was badly in need of some money, times were hard, the dirty thirties you know, and not much work for a carpenter that was so talented in his craft. Mr. Murphy, I always called him that because I was taught that we respected our elders, well, he kept that carpenter busy with the desk. Some gossips say your grandfather had him add secret compartments, hidden drawers and did most of the other woodwork here in the mansion. That work continued until the economy got better."

Benjamin looked at the built in bookcases, the carved wood around the fireplace, beautiful cabinets and the wooden floor with runner rugs. Even the small couch and chairs around the fireplace had wood trim on them. This was basically a man's room.

Pulling the key from his pocket, Benjamin unlocked the desk and removed the ring of keys. "Let's explore the rest of the house, and if there is time, we can come back here and see about hidden compartments in the desk. I need to look at the photographs; I need to know where I came from. You wouldn't happen to know why all these years my dad and grandfather never got in touch with one another do you. My dad wouldn't talk about it at all and I assumed my grandparents died some tragic death."

"Sorry, no I don't. Like you said, it just wasn't talked about. Oh yes, there was always the bussing around the local gossips, but I was too young and one thing you learn being raised with the sheriff is you don't take as gospel everything you hear." She smiled at him. "Let's go to the attic! There are hundreds of things to see from years before your grandfather. This mansion was built before your grandfather moved here, and they kept just about everything. Even some of the clothes and we got to wear them during the pageants celebrating the centennials and things like that. There is even an old baby buggy made of wicker. Your grandmother use to let me push it around. There was a doll that had the most beautiful face, but I had to be careful because it was breakable. It was a fun place to play in on a rainy day. You never know what you'll find in places like an attic."

How right she was.

CHAPTER FOUR

Benjamin was surprised when he opened the door to the attic and it didn't squeak. He looked over at JC, "I don't believe it. Even the hinges on this door are oiled."

"I told you John loves this place as his own. Over the years, he created a schedule of maintenance for everything. See how clean and organized this floor is." She stepped into the room and with her arms stretched out moved slowly in a circle.

Even with only the light from the windows, Benjamin was amazed at the order of the room that covered the length of the mansion. He turned and seeing multiple light switches, flipped on one that happened to be the main light.

"The lighting is divided into three sections, so lights that can be turned on in each area as needed. I use to play up here at times. I loved it with all the clothes and old furniture." JC smiled as she thought back over the years.

Benjamin stood still and let his eyes wander over everything that was in his field of vision. He was absolutely amazed that so many things were kept, and that they were in excellent shape, not just junk thrown up here to get out of the way.

Some were definitely antiques that would bring in a pretty penny.

Taking his hand, JC pulled him over to the space she thought he would be interested in. "This is all the stuff that was your dads. There is even a sealed box that has 'school papers and rewards' written on it. Your grandma always said if any box was sealed, I couldn't get into it."

The two stopped in front of child size desk, behind it were shelves with boxes on it, clothes hung up in clear bags in order of sizes. Plastic boxes stacked on the floor held polished shoes. What must have been some special toys were in clear totes with lids on them.

Many emotions were running through Benjamin's mind as he picked up various items and ran his hands over them. *My dad never told me about all of these things. Did he have fun with them? Which ones were his favorites? Oh my gosh, there's a train set just like mine, and the basket balls...*

Part of Benjamin felt a little anger at not knowing about this part of his dad's life. *What was so secretive that he couldn't share what must have been a perfect childhood? Even his high school years show that he was involved in sports and seems to have been popular.*

Seeing how silent Benjamin had become, JC touched his arm lightly. "Do you want to stop for the day?"

"No, no. Let's just walk by everything and come up some other time, there is so much to see and discuss about the whole mansion. I really enjoy hearing what you know about the mansion, or should I say, my dad's home."

The two spent about another hour browsing in the attic and then decided to go back downstairs. "I think I'll take the box about dad's school and the one next to it that says scrapbook. I wonder if he always had the analytical mind of an attorney or if he had desires to be, oh, I don't know, a math teacher." He picked up the first box.

"I'll get the scrapbook one," JC stooped to pick it up.

"It might be heavy; I'll come back later and get it. I don't want you to hurt yourself carrying the box."

"You forgot that as a policewoman, I work out and am very strong, this weight is fine. But thanks for being concerned." She walked toward the door.

Benjamin laughed, "I guess part of a lawyer's instinct is knowing law suits come from situations just as this, picking up a box that is too heavy, and the next thing a person's back is out of whack and they can't work. You get the picture, plus, I'd hate for you to injure yourself." He balanced the box with one arm, shut off the lights and closed the door softly behind him.

"Where do you want to put the boxes to go through them, in the den?" JC asked as they reached the bottom of the last flight of steps.

"Sounds like a perfect place to me. I'm getting hungry, how about you? There is way too much food in the refrigerator for just me." He set the box down on the floor next to a coffee table by the couch.

"You must be getting a little tired of me being around and there is so much for you to do plus check in with your office." She had placed her box next to Benjamin's and brushed her hands together, then wiped them on her pants.

"I can do that when you leave. The office would have called or text me if it there was anything urgent. There weren't any real complicated cases pending when I decided to come here. In the meantime, I enjoy your companionship very much. Now, do you want to raid the refrigerator, go out to eat, or have something ordered in?" He raised his right eyebrow with the question.

"Your grandpa use to do that."

"Do what?" Benjamin looked at her with a quizzical look.

"Raise his right eyebrow when he asked a question that gave a person more than one choice." JC responded with a laugh. "And, for the record, I'm for grazing through the refrigerator."

The two sauntered to the kitchen, with JC again pointing out some piece of information she thought Benjamin would want to know, like the chair the haute over weight Mrs. Olson got stuck in.

After eating, they returned to the den and Benjamin opened the box with 'school papers and rewards' on it. They laughed over the cute class pictures when his dad was little, the year with the two front teeth missing and a huge grin on his face, and comments from teachers on his report cards. Most of the time, his dad was referred to as 'Billy', not William as teachers would have to do today on all correspondence to parents or for the files. William was a very good student until, the senior year of high school, then grades began sliding down, and the notes were of William being late, assignments not completed, and one of alcohol on his breath when he was suspended from classes for three days.

Benjamin leaned back against the couch. "I think I've had enough for tonight. Part of me wants to keep going to know about dad, but I need to stop and digest all of this. What turned dad from an 'A' student to almost flunking? A girl? The wrong crowd? What?"

JC stood up and stretched. "Sorry, I don't know. You can ponder that in your dreams, I need to go home and refresh myself on the lesson for tomorrow."

Putting the lid back on the box, Benjamin inquired, "Tomorrow, what lesson?"

"My church has Sunday school classes for all ages and the adult class is studying the Book of Luke. It's very interesting. We have a study guide we use. The class starts at 9:45 and stops at 10:45. The preaching service starts at 11:00. Would you like to come? I'll pick you up if you don't mind riding in my Jeep." JC paused with her hand on the door knob.

"If you don't mind, I'd like to attend. Did my dad and grandparents attend services at that church too?"

"Yes, they did. I'll come by say, 9:15? The ladies aid department usually has rolls and coffee before the classes start and we get to chit chat a bit with each other." She opened the door to the porch.

"Thanks again for your help, JC." Benjamin said as she went down the steps to her Jeep.

She waved at him, "No problem, see you tomorrow. Sleep well." Sliding into the seat she shut the door and put on her seatbelt.

Benjamin watched until the Jeep pulled onto the road and vanished from his view. He closed the door and locked it. He liked JC. For some reason he felt like he had always known her. She was comfortable and fun to be around. Suddenly he felt alone and the house so quiet.

He glanced at his watch, time to check his email and then perhaps look in the other box.

CHAPTER FIVE

Promptly at 9:15, JC pulled to a stop in front of the mansion. She wasn't surprised to see Benjamin sitting in a chair waiting for her. What did catch her attention was the Bible on his lap.

Rapidly descending the steps, Benjamin opened the Jeep's door. "Hi, I'm Benjamin Murphy. I didn't know JC had a twin sister who is a model."

"Funny, Benjamin. Get in or we'll be late for church." She smiled at him but pleased with his comment.

Sliding into the seat, Benjamin turned toward her, "Seriously, your dress is very becoming, that shade of blue matches your eyes. I've only seen you in uniform or jeans, working clothes. I really like your hair down framing your face."

Blushing like a school girl and slightly embarrassed, "Thank you. I like to wear a dress for church."

As they drove, JC pointed out some places of interest in which his grandfather had been instrumental in building, such as the daycare and expansion to the library.

The church was located in the center of town. It was the largest church. There was a small Catholic church at the other end of the town. JC found a spot along the curb to park. She left the small parking lot close to the church for the elderly or those who were handicapped.

Benjamin got out of the Jeep opened JC's door and gave her a hand to assist her out. He noticed with her high heels on her head came up to his chin.

"Thank you." JC wasn't accustomed to this at all, but she liked the courtesy he showed to her.

Turning, Benjamin took in the huge stone building that during the years had been added to, but done in keeping with the original design. It had been modernized to include central heating and air conditioning, and an attached building he assumed held classrooms and the kitchen.

Benjamin offered his arm to JC as they slowly walked to the entrance where people were being greeted by those around the door. JC made the introductions, and skipping the coffee and rolls, they went to the basement of the church where the adult classes were held. After an interesting discussion of Luke, the class was too soon over. She was surprised that Benjamin was so familiar with the scriptures.

As they went up the stairs to the sanctuary, Benjamin looked at the picture in the vestibule of Jesus at the door. The small gold sign under it said, 'In memory of Margaret and Carl Smith'.

Lightly touching the frame, JC in a soft voice said, "My grandparents purchased that when my parents died. They said

Jesus had knocked on the door to my parent's hearts and they let Him in and are in heaven with Jesus." Her eyes grew a little misty and she dabbed at her eyes with a tissue, "I don't even remember them."

Benjamin reached for her hand and the two walked through the open double doors.

Impressed with the beautiful stained glass windows, Benjamin walked over by one and read the small plaque under it that said, 'Donated by Willard and Elizabeth Murphy in memory of William Murphy'. *In memory of? Did they think he was dead or thought of his dad as dead when they paid for this expensive window showing Christ with a flock of sheep behind Him?* Benjamin needed to find some answers, but who had them? Would he find them in the box at home? It would have to wait until he got back to the mansion. He couldn't ask her to leave now, and would the answer be there anyway?

He slowly walked back to JC's side where she was conversing with the usher. She introduced Benjamin to him and taking a bulletin they walked to the front of the church and sat in the second pew. Benjamin wondered if she always sat here.

They sat quietly while the organist played prelude music and then the choir took their seats. The service began.

Reverend John Haroldson stood and smiled at them all. "Today, I'm using scripture from the Book of Luke. I love how Jesus taught, and although the adult class will get to this chapter later, I felt lead to share this with you today. Luke 6:35-38."

JC and Benjamin followed along in their Bibles.

For some reason, verses 37 and 38 stood out for Benjamin. Verse 37 *Judge not and ye shall not be judged: condemn not, and ye shall not be condemned: forgive, and ye shall be forgiven: Verse 38 Give, and it shall be given unto you; good measure, pressed down, and shaken together, and running over, shall men give into your bosom. For with the same measure that ye mete withal it shall be measured to you again.*

Benjamin could hear the voice of the Reverend in the background but his mind was on those scriptures. *When he came to this town, he had been angry, not only with his dad, but his grandparents. Why didn't they tell him he had family? But he also knew they were all generous, giving to charity and to the people they employed.*

He was startled out of his thoughts as JC poked him in the side with her elbow as the congregation was standing to sing the closing hymn. His rich baritone voice blended well with hers. He looked over at her feeling glad to be sharing this time with her.

As they slowly exited the church, Benjamin was anxious to get back to the house and see what else he could discover. Somehow, he felt like he had been cheated out of some precious family experiences. What could have happened to cause such a divide?

* * *

"I hate to monopolize your time, JC, I realize you have other things to do but would you care to have lunch with me and go through the other box this afternoon?" Benjamin had unhooked his seat belt and was looking at her. *Maybe if something does show up, she can explain in more detail.*

"That depends what you have in mind for lunch." Laughing at him as she too un did her seat belt without waiting for his response opened the door.

"I'll take that as a yes," Benjamin said getting out of the Jeep, "I think there is plenty in the refrigerator to feast on."

Once again, working as a team they fixed a meal, and picking up their glasses of ice tea, went to the den to check out the scrapbook box.

Benjamin stood to one side as JC entered the room. She removed her high heels and tucking one leg under her took a seat on the leather couch, her skirt flowing softly over the cushion.

Taking off his suit jacket, Benjamin sat down next to her and pulled the duct tape from around the box, and taking a deep breath wondered what they would find, he took off the lid.

As Benjamin removed all six scrapbooks from the box and placed them on the table he noticed they were numbered one through six.

Picking up the first book, Benjamin leaned back on the seat and opened it. He flipped through it observing newspaper clippings, pictures and typed comments then went back to the first page and moved the book so they both could see the contents. Unfolding the newspaper, he saw the wreckage of a boat on the water. The headlines read 'TRAGIC DEATHS ON THE RIVER'.

"Today the town of Freedomville mourns the loss Margaret and Carl Smith, William Murphy, and childhood friend Bobby James. The body of William Murphy hasn't been found and the search is still being continued.

This has been the worst river accident the town has ever known. The police are continuing the investigation of what caused this tragedy."

Benjamin stopped reading aloud, and let the book rest on their laps. *This didn't compute. If his dad died that day, then who was his dad? Was there another son out there? Was he an illegitimate child?*

Remaining quiet, JC was assessing the wound that was being opened. *She knew her parents had died in the boating accident, but she had been a baby, loved by her grandparents and no one talked about it around her. What caused that fateful accident?*

Benjamin looked at her, "I don't know what to say. Are you okay?"

JC nodded her head.

"Let's keep reading then." Ben picked the album back up.

The two of them read through all six of the scrapbooks that held a lot of repeat items, the death announcements, the church bulletins from the funeral and memorial service for William, whose body had never been found, even after the river had been dragged by knowledgeable rescue men.

Benjamin and JC stood up and stretched. They had been sitting for a long time.

They had marked some of the pages with sticky notes to check on certain details that they wanted some clarity on. Would they find any after all these years?

Benjamin walked over to the window and looked out into the starless night. He ran his hand through his hair, turned and looked at JC. "Do I belong here? None of this makes any sense unless, the reason they didn't find the body of William Murphy is because he didn't die in the boat crash. But then, why didn't he come forth and tell someone? My God, how my grandparents must have grieved." He stopped and went to one of the books and flipped through it until he found the article he was searching for.

"Rumors around town say that William Murphy had been doing a lot of drinking and recently been expelled from school for three days for having alcohol on his breath after the noon break. He and his friend, Bobby James have been seen on the river most days after school in a recently purchased twenty foot cruiser speeding and making waves that interfered with others' fishing."

Benjamin put the book down and leaned against the desk and looked over at JC who was putting on her heels. "How come you and your grandparents were so close to mine? Didn't they hate them? Come on, their son was responsible for your parents death! You must think I'm terrible person. I don't know how I'm supposed to be here. Did my dad survive or not? Is that why he wouldn't talk about his past?"

JC walked over to Benjamin and put her hand on his arm. "I don't have the answers. All I remember was being loved by my grandparents and your grandparents. No one knows what happened on the river that day. My family always went to church, and I was taught that Jesus forgives. Hate destroys. Two families grieved together, and in doing so, let those deaths bring some peace to them. I hold no animosity toward you. Why would I? Would that bring them back to life? Remember the scripture from this morning, judge not and forgive? Just think, we are the last of two families. I don't know about you, but I don't want a return of the 'Hatfield's vs. the Mc Coy's."

She backed away. "I need to leave. I'm tired and I'm on the early shift this week. You still have the safe to go through and the desk to explore to see if they hold any more answers for you."

Benjamin gently touched her arm. "I hate to impose on your time, but would you stop by after your shift is over? I really want you here on this investigation. Tomorrow I need to check in with my office and then I'll go through some more files and I would like to have your input on anything that I find."

"I need to work out when my shift is finished." JC responded as she picked up her purse that also held her badge and gun from the hall table.

"No problem. How about grilled steak and a baked potato to eat as I share whatever I've found?" Benjamin smiled at her, happy that she would come back again.

"That has the distinct sound of a bribing an officer to me." She laughed. "But I accept."

"Ah, but you will be off duty by that time. By the way, what time do you want to eat?" Benjamin followed as she walked to the door.

Turning around to face him, "Does 5:00 sound okay to you? I'll be pushing it a bit. I'll call you if I get waylaid on a case." She slipped the keys from her purse.

"Fine, see you tomorrow, and, JC, thanks for being here." Benjamin had a very sincere look on his face.

She just nodded, "Toodle do," and with a wave of her hand, went to her Jeep.

Benjamin stayed on the front veranda and watched the Jeep disappear. He felt lonely with her gone. With a sigh, he went and sat on one of the chairs. He was mentally going through all the scrapbooks. What was he missing?

CHAPTER SIX

Hours later, he rubbed his eyes, he had absorbed all his mind could take for one evening, but he was physically restless. Benjamin walked to the kitchen and retrieved a soda from the refrigerator. Slowly, he walked back through the rooms, touching the furniture lightly, picturing a family he didn't know sitting there. He looked more closely at the painted portraits of his grandparents and a young boy that he assumed was his father. Benjamin and his dad looked like brothers. Even his grandfather's picture looked like an older version of Benjamin and William.

Going back to the den, he settled into the desk chair and leaned back. *The paper said William was presumed drowned. Yet, all the facts show that he didn't and he was living proof that his dad had survived. There were just too many questions unanswered.*

Looking at the desk top, the odd, big, old fashioned key on the ring caught his attention. It was labeled: safe. Picking up the ring, Benjamin went to the huge ancient safe concealed behind a wooden wall. *That was probably another work project for that man who built the desk. It was a good thing the lawyer told him about it or he never would have looked for it.*

Evidently, even JC doesn't know about the safe or she would have mentioned it.

The huge safe was bolted to the floor and must have been used for business purposes at one time. Inserting the thick heavy key, Ben unlocked the iron door with a painted design like a crest on it. It gave a slight creaking sound as he opened it. He made a mental note to spray some oil on the hinges. A slight musty smell emanated from it. Benjamin was surprised to find on one side, another locked door. There were some shelves and cubbyholes in the main part of the safe. He moved the keys around on the ring until he found the one that fit that second door.

Benjamin hesitated. Part of him was curious as to what was in there, maybe the key to his past, but yet he was slightly apprehensive about it, a feeling that he might be opening up a can of worms he didn't want to deal with. He took a deep breath; he hadn't become a top notch attorney without taking chances.

The lock made a clicking sound as he turned the key. He pulled gently on the small handle. There was an old fashion brown accordion pleated folder so full it strained the laces it was tied with. Slowly, Benjamin removed it and carried it to the desk. He had a gut feeling this might hold some answers.

Going back to the safe, he swiftly perused the other contents. There were records of past business dealings, taxes, property deeds and personal records like birth certificates. Attorney Jensen had the current ones in his office and bank statements that he had been taking care of in the past two years. He would look at those later: right now he felt pulled to see the contents of the folder on the desk.

Pulling one end of the tie, he lifted the folder flap and saw labeled manila folders. Glancing at the labels, he saw: Police Report, Rescue Divers, Insurance Report, Detective Report, William.

Benjamin removed the **Police Report** folder first. He quickly paged through it and didn't find any more information than they had gathered from the scrapbooks.

Rescue Divers mainly held the information of how the dragging and diving had produced nothing to identify William, but Bobby James and body parts and clothing of the Smith family were found to identify them.

The **Insurance Report** basically ruled it an accident due to a faulty throttle control and paid off the cruiser to Willard, and a huge payment to JC, for the loss of her parents. It was to be put in a trust fund until she turned thirty five, unless her grandparents who were given guardianship of her needed some finances for her schooling. *Um, I wonder if she knows about this or didn't feel it was any of my business?*

The **Detective Report** went from that date to two years ago and showed information on his dad and himself! *What? His grandfather had engaged private detectives and knew he was alive! Why didn't his grandfather contact them? Did his dad know?*

Benjamin got up and paced the floor. Part of him was angry, part of him was sad. *He could have been part of a family! Who made the decision NOT to tell him and why?*

He went back to the desk and grabbed the last folder: **William**. Inside were letters with the envelopes stapled to the top. Some were on scraps of paper and a few toward the end were neatly typed.

Picking up the first letter that was written with pencil on a scrap of paper, were just two lines, "Dad, I'm alive. Don't tell anyone. I'll write later. William"

Benjamin turned it face down and picked up the next one. This long letter was written in ink, the old type of pen where you inserted the ink cartridge in it. There were some smear marks on it like tears had fallen on it. *Were they his dad's tears, or his grandfathers?*

"Dear Dad and Mom,

I have to tell you what happened on that dreadful day on the river. As you know, I was on suspension from school for drinking. You don't know how I disliked some of those teachers who made fun of me because you were so prominent in the community. They kept calling me 'little rich boy'.

Bobby's family always drank and that day of the accident, we stopped over there for lunch and his dad told us to have a beer, that no one would be the wiser and what right did the school have to tell him what his son could drink. I <u>promise</u> you Dad, I didn't drink any. I had a soda. Honest and you know I've never lied to you. Then Bobby and I decided to go over to the dock and get our cruiser and have some fun since we couldn't be at school.

Coming from a poor family and not having a boat like ours, Bobby wanted to be at the controls. I just told him to go slow since there are so many bends in the river that you never know what is around them. I went down the steps to get some more sodas and I felt the cruiser speeding up. I was going up the steps to tell him to slow down, when Bobby started yelling, 'It's stuck, the throttle is stuck!' The cruiser was flying and the bend was coming around, and I didn't think he would make it, that we'd slam into the bank. I hollered at him, "Jump Bobby!"

Bobby hung onto the wheel and we made the corner but there was a small boat the Smith family owned stalled in the water. I knew we were going to hit it, and I jumped overboard.

Dad, I can still hear the thunderous sound of the crash and I felt it under the water. When I came up to the surface, the cruiser had smashed through the boat and into some trees on the bank. The motor was still roaring.

I couldn't see anyone else, I kept diving and looking. There were broken parts of the boats all over in the water bumping into me. I was exhausted and climbed up on the bank to get my breath.

That's when it hit me: it was our cruiser and everyone would assume I was at the controls. If I said Bobby was, they would say I was lying to get out of it. I wasn't in school because of having that one stupid beer and they would assume we both had been drinking. I would be blamed for all of this! I couldn't stay here, knowing three people were dead. And little Janice, losing both of her parents: my heart breaks for her. Take care of her, please. Oh Dad and Mom, if they didn't put me in jail, I would be always be walking around town with an invisible 'M' on my forehead for murder.

I can't do that to you both. Our family has been a pillar of this community for so long, helping it grow, we were here from the beginning. It will be better for you if everyone thinks I'm dead.

Don't look for me, I'll send you a note from time to time, but I can never come home.

I love you, William"

Benjamin let the letter fall from his hands unto the desk. There were tears in his eyes. Now he knew why his dad would never go on a boat or a cruise ship, and insisted he knew how to swim. He had a lot of why's racing through his mind.

Leaning forward, he turned that letter over and placed it in the pile and took the next one. It was dated two years later. There was no return address and the postmark was smudged, and not discernible.

Benjamin swiftly went through the short one page letter that basically said he had a job and was going to night school. He was fine and hoped they were too.

Going through the rest of the letters which were always postmarked from different cities and never with a return address on them, were basically the same, just telling them that he was fine and not to worry, except for the last two.

"Dear Folks,

I just married a wonderful person. We are so much alike. She is an only child and was adopted. I told her I was orphaned. Sorry, but I have say that to explain not having a family. I will always have to keep that a secret. She is so loving I know she would want to find you. I just can't go through all of that. I guess I am a coward.

I also want you to know that I've completed my education and am working at a very prestigious job. You would approve.

Love, William."

Then Benjamin picked up the last letter written the year he was born. He could see it was postmarked New York.

"Dear Mom and Dad,

I just had to tell you that this morning I held my newborn son. He is the most beautiful baby I have ever seen. We named him Benjamin. I cried at the wonder of this life I held in my arms. My darling wife is doing fine. I have been very blessed.

Love,
William and family."

Benjamin's throat was tight. He got up and paced the room, he was angry that they didn't give him a chance to make the decision to know his grandparents. He went back to the desk and reread the last letter and put his head down on his arms and cried. There were tears for lost years of family, tears for the hurt that his dad went through and tears for his grandparents who lost their only child.

Sitting up, he wiped his eyes. He really had no complaints about the life he had. Mom and dad had been good to him, loved him dearly. They saw that he had the best education available and left him with a very lucrative and well known business, but they cheated him out of knowing his grandparents.

What else would he find out about the past?

CHAPTER SEVEN

The sun streaming through the white curtains woke Benjamin from a night of dreams. More like nightmares of boats smashing, funerals, and crying people with broken hearts and a baby wondering where her mommy and daddy were.

He put his hand over his eyes to shut out the light and laid there quietly reassessing all he had read the night before. One: His dad wasn't the cause of the cruiser crashing into the Smith boat. Two: He wasn't illegitimate. Three: His grandparents had never disowned him.

Benjamin sighed, *such a waste of long lost years when they could have been together for birthdays, holidays and for what, some gossip?*

He untangled himself from the sheets and sat on the edge of the bed and ran his hand through his hair. He glanced over at the clock. 7:00 AM. Time to get a move on, he needed to check in with his office and he was curious about the rest of the things in the safe.

Making his bed, he grabbed some clothes and headed for the shower.

Completing his morning routine, he pulled on a pair of brown shorts and a light tan polo shirt and slipped on a pair of loafers. Time for breakfast.

Pushing the on button of the coffee maker, Benjamin was surprised to hear a tap on the kitchen door. Opening it he found old John standing there.

"Good Morning, John. Come in."

"Morning, Mr. Murphy. Thank you."

"I was just going to have some coffee and breakfast. Will you join me?" Benjamin gestured at the coffee maker.

"No thank you, I've already had my breakfast. I was wondering if you would like to go with me today and see some of the other property that you own, there are two working farms close by. The foreman for each farm and their families live there and take care of the place like it is their own. The paper records for each one are at their office and on the computer. Since your grandfather passed away, Mr. Jensen has the monthly reports sent to his office."

"Why I certainly would like that. Thanks for asking me." Benjamin took a mug out of the cupboard, "Would you join me with a cup of coffee while I have some breakfast?"

"No thank you, Mr. Murphy. Your grandfather was an early riser and would have been finished by now. He and I spent many hours at this table discussing his properties." A shadow of sadness crossed his face.

"John, please call me Benjamin. There's no need for formality between us. Now tell me about the first place we will visit." Benjamin turned to put a bagel into the toaster. Reaching into the refrigerator for the cream cheese and coffee creamer, he set them on the counter.

"John, have a seat." Benjamin gestured at a chair.

"No thanks, Mr. Murphy, I'll go wait outside."

The toaster popped up and Benjamin reached for the bagel.

"No, please, have a seat. I'll just be a minute and we can leave." Benjamin quickly began to spread cream cheese on the bagel.

John remained standing by the door with his hat in his hand.

"Tell me, John. Were my grandparents happy? Were you working here when the boat accident happened?"

"They were always happy; they had a great love and were devoted to each other. The house was always full of people visiting or some community activity being held here." He paused a moment. "They were hard workers and didn't ask anything of us that they wouldn't do. They were very well respected in the county and the state." John looked down at his feet, took a breath and continued.

"Yes, I was working here when the boat accident happened. So sad, never finding the body took a huge toll on them, especially your grandmother. She died two years before your grandfather. She was rather frail then." John's eyes grew misty. "I think it was hard on her not knowing what happened to her boy."

"So, how is the community explaining me?" Benjamin poured some coffee in a 'to go' cup.

John slowly turned the rim of his old hat through his work worn hands then looked up at Benjamin. "Some folks think you are an impostor out to steal Mr. Willard's money. Others think that since William's body was never found, you might be kin."

Stepping closer to the older man, Benjamin looked him in the eyes and said softly, "And you, John, who do you, think I am?"

"Time will tell, Mr. Murphy." John slowly turned around, put on his hat, and opened the door stepping out onto the back porch.

Benjamin picked up his cup and followed the old gentleman. He could feel John's animosity toward him and it hurt. He could understand why, but having his integrity questioned was uncomfortable. Since Mr. Jensen and the police department knew who he was, he guessed everyone else thought he was illegitimate.

He reached the truck just as John was opening the door.

"Wait, John. Come back into the house. I want to show you something." Benjamin turned around and retraced his steps to the house. Holding the door for John to go through, then Benjamin lead the way to the study.

"Take that chair in front of the desk, John. I want to show you something I discovered in the safe last night." Sitting down on the desk chair, Benjamin opened the middle drawer and removed a folder from the file. Selecting the last three letters that his dad had mailed to his grandfather, he slid them across the desk to John.

Placing his hat on his knee, John reached into his shirt pocket for his reading glasses and put them on. He took the first letter off the desk, his lips moving as he read but no sound was uttered. From time to time, he looked over at Benjamin, but didn't say a word. He leaned forward, putting the first letter back and took the next one and read that.

Benjamin tamped some tobacco from the pouch into his pipe and lit it.

John glanced up at this action of Benjamin but didn't say anything and read the short last note.

Benjamin had leaned back into the old wooden chair and tented his fingers as he tried to read something from John's face as John read the letters. All he noticed was the old man's expression had softened.

Placing the last letter on top of the other two, in a pensive motion, John took off his glasses and put them back into his pocket.

Benjamin sucked in another pull of the pipe. "Mr. Jensen has reports from a private investigating firm that documents my birth and the fact that my grandfather had been watching my dad and me from afar. Now, John, who do you think I am and how do you think I feel being cheated all of these years from knowing the two people who lived in this home?"

A tear slowly crept down the weathered face from the corner of John's eye. In a voice choked with emotion, "I worked with Will, that's what I called him, when he first came to town with just his new degree. We worked the fields, we delivered calves, fought a lightning fire that hit the barn, and we survived the crash in the thirties. Will and Elizabeth lived in just part of the mansion to save money. He seemed to have a gift in making all his endeavors pay well."

He looked up at Benjamin, "I was with him the day your dad was born, and he was like a brother to me, we didn't have any secrets, but he never, ever mentioned to me that William was alive. Never!"

Wiping the lone tear away with the back of his hand, he shook his head. "Didn't he trust me? Me? He offered me other jobs with more prestige, but I loved working with the land and animals. I managed those he managed the other businesses. But to never tell me, the one person who knew all of his business, something as important as this: his only child was alive? Why keep it a secret? For all he did for this community, he should have told them the truth, people would have understood, if they didn't, tough." John pulled a huge old blue bandana type hankie from his back pocket and blew his nose.

"Oh, poor Elizabeth, losing her only son and never able to hold her only grandson. Did she even know about him? John shook his head slowly back and forth. "But she poured all that love into little Janice and treated her like she was her own little one."

Benjamin took another large file from the drawer and placed it in front of John. "This is just one of many that show the investigations my grandfather had on dad and me, John. I don't need this money or property of my grandfather. Dad and I built a highly lucrative business. We are well known in New York as reputable attorneys."

Placing his pipe down on the large ceramic ashtray, Benjamin looked over at the old gentleman. In a dejected tone of voice, "John, all I wanted was to have a history, a family. I have no one. No one. All everyone else thinks about is money. Money. Would you trade any of your family, hugs from the children, for money?"

Shaking his head, Benjamin went on. "Back in New York I am invited to parties just to have their daughters fostered on me. So many women don't really care about anything but to be married to a respectable someone with money. To belong to clubs and travel in style."

Leaning back into the comfortable old chair, "Do you really think I would come out to this community to be ridiculed either as an impostor or illegitimate person for some more money?"

It was then that Benjamin noticed a change in John.

John's face was ashen; sweat covered his forehead as he clutched at his chest and whispered, "He didn't trust me," and collapsed onto the floor.

CHAPTER EIGHT

JC heard the 911 call on the squad radio for an ambulance needed at the Murphy mansion.

"I'm just a few blocks away, I'll go." She spoke into the mike as she turned on the flashing red and blue lights.

In a minute, she pulled into the long driveway and came to a fast stop a couple of car lengths past the front steps, allowing room for the ambulance that was just turning off the road into the lane.

Taking the porch steps two at a time, she didn't knock, just barged into the house. "Benjamin? Where are you?"

"In the study," was his terse reply.

She found Benjamin doing CPR on John. Turning to the medics coming into the house, she gestured to them. "Bring the gurney in here."

The two medics worked swiftly to stabilize John, got him into the ambulance and left for the hospital, with the siren screaming and lights flashing.

JC and Benjamin followed closely behind in the squad car.

At the hospital, they questioned Benjamin on what had transpired while John was whisked off to the inner medical wonders of the hospital.

After JC left to finish her shift, Benjamin nervously walked the length of the hallway back and forth feeling responsible for John's collapse. He was so engrossed in his thoughts he didn't notice the swinging door open and Dr. Greenwood come through, but he stopped when he felt the doctor's hand on his arm.

"Is John alright? I should have never shared some things with him. It's my entire fault. I upset him with some paper work I let him read."

"Sit down, Mr. Murphy isn't it? John has a history of myocardial infarction, or in layman's terms, I should say John had a heart attack. He has had one before and refuses to have a bypass done so we have been trying to treat the problem with drugs and the common aspirin. Currently we have him stabilized but this might just convince him if he wants to continue doing the things he loves, working with animals and nature, he needs this surgery. This episode could just as well happen during his sleep. Please do not think you were responsible." The doctor stood up and touched Benjamin's shoulder.

"And you young man, relax or you might become my next patient." The doctor's pager beeped. "Duty calls. We are keeping John for observation and maybe we can convince him to have the surgery. His son is coming over, so we will see."

Waving his hand at Benjamin, Dr. Greenwood went back through the swinging doors.

Benjamin sat there with his elbows on his knees, holding his head in his hands contemplating on what to do. It wasn't exactly the position a prominent attorney from New York would like to have photographed, but at the moment, that was the last thing on Benjamin's mind. Was this what his grandfather worked hard for to make money so there could be this much confusion?

Benjamin didn't hear but felt the presence of JC. He looked up, then stood up and took her in his arms and held her tight. The warmth and strength of her renewed him. He stepped back and smiled, "Lady, did you know hugging a police officer with all your weapons and paraphernalia on is very uncomfortable?"

Looking up at him, JC smiled, "I'll take your word for it since I've never hugged a policeman in full uniform."

Holding hands, they walked down the corridor. "I take it John is doing okay?"

"Yes, I just spoke with the doctor and he said John has had a heart attack before and he hopes he can talk him into by-pass surgery this time." Benjamin paused, "I want to stop at the desk and leave a note for his son that I will pay for any medical expenses."

JC's laughter caused Benjamin to turn and look at her with a quizzical expression. "Ben, Ben," she covered her mouth to contain her laughter in the quiet hallway, "Don't you know that John is a very rich man and doesn't need your money?

Your grandfather invested a portion of John's wages for him and he is about as rich as your grandfather was. John had the money and your grandfather had the land, buildings, and animals that John loved to work with." She stood there with a smile on her face at his surprise with this information.

"That doesn't detract from the fact I did show him the letters and he reacted to them with this heart attack. Now what can I do to rectify it?" Benjamin inquired.

"Well, for starters," She linked her arm through his as they walked out of the hospital, "We will stop by my place so I can change clothes. Second, we go to your home and you can feed me, you always have more food than one person can consume and let me in on the letters."

"Officer, I approve your suggestion." Benjamin opened the Jeep's door for her. "All in favor so signify by saying, Aye." They both burst out laughing.

What they didn't notice was John's grandson, Tim, looking out the window of his grandfather's room watching the happy couple. *It's not fair. I've asked her out and asked her out and she won't give me the time of day. But this supposedly grandson of Mr. Murphy, Mr. Hot Shot lawyer from New York shows up and she is all full of smiles. If dad or granddad would just give me some money I'd shake the dirt of this town off my shoes. Why should I have to work? If I'm not responsible and hold down a job, I lose all my inheritance when either grandpa or dad dies. They have it all sewn up in a trust fund. They would rather give it to charity than me, their own flesh and blood.* Turning around he could see if his dad was still next to his grandpa talking with the nurse. He wiped his hand over his over his mouth, *man, he needed a drink.*

Yeah, he'd just go down to the bar and have a drink or two. Reaching into his pocket, he pulled out a few bills, *or maybe by a bottle of cheap Old Crow Whiskey. Dad won't miss me.*

* * *

Taking the last bite of her salad, JC leaned back, contented into her chair. "What was going on in the den when John collapsed?"

Pushing his plate away, Benjamin leaned forward, placing his arms on the table, toyed with the salt shaker. "It all started when he came to the back door and wanted to show me one of the farms." He then told her all that had transpired.

"Can I read the letters too?" She was full of curiosity. *It would be nice to see something and not just the word of Mr. Jensen that Benjamin was Mr. Murphy's grandson.*

"Of course, I'm actually interested in what you have to say about it. I was elated in one way, but on the other hand, sad and angry to be cheated out of a family." Benjamin slowly shook his head back and forth, "And to think all these years people have blamed my dad for the accident." He sighed, looking up at her, "Forgive me for being so self centered. You lost your parents, as least I had mine and they were good ones.

Slowly she stood up and walked over to Benjamin, leaning down she put her arms around his shoulder, resting her chin on his head. "We can't waste our lives over what we can't change and had no control over. As my grandpa would say when I would bring up the loss of my mom and dad, 'be thankful for what you have and live your life so they would be proud of you'. Then he would hug me or mess up my hair and we'd go fishing or something.

Benjamin took her hands in his and held them against his chest. They remained that way, each silent in their own thoughts.

Then releasing his hold on her, Benjamin stood up, turned around and took her in his arms, leaned his head down and kissed her gently on her lips. "Thank you."

JC wrapped her arms around him and returned his kiss. "You're welcome."

Standing still in the quiet kitchen looking into each other eyes, the emotions of new feelings were emanating from both of them.

They both jumped as the phone rang. Keeping his arm around her waist, he reached for the phone.

"Hello."

"Mr. Murphy, Harold Hermanson here, John's son. I hope I haven't disturbed you but I wanted to let you know dad is convalescing and wishes to see you."

"Of course, but I don't want to excite him. He has been through a lot today. Do you think this is a good idea?"

Chuckling, Harold said, "You evidently don't know my dad. When dad says 'come', no one says no, just when."

Benjamin glanced over at the wall clock, "I can leave now."

"Fine. He is in room 324. I'll be here." The phone clicked as Harold hung up.

Ben put the receiver back and looked down at JC, "Want to join me?"

"You think you were going to leave me here when John has something to say to you? Besides I just declared myself your designated chauffeur. Let's go."

* * *

Tim sat in his truck taking swigs from his bottle of Old Crow Whiskey when he saw his JC and Benjamin enter the hospital parking lot. He slid down in the seat so he could just look over the edge of his window. He watched as they exited the Jeep. It irritated him when he saw them embrace and then hold hands as they walked toward the hospital entrance.

Placing his hands on the steering wheel he growled, "What's the fancy dude think he's doing cozying up to JC? She's my gal."

He sat there, his brain getting foggy as he plotted what he could do to convince Janice Caroline he was the man for her. *Why dad and grandpa would give him some money early if she married him. They always did have a soft spot for her.* Taking a drink from the now half empty whiskey bottle, he decided to stay put and wait until they left the hospital, then he's follow her home. She just needed a little time to know he was a better man than the city slicker. Screwing the cap on the bottle, he placed it next to him but kept his hand on the neck of it like a kid with a favorite stuffed toy. A few minutes later, he totally succumbed to the alcohols' effects.

* * *

Benjamin and JC stopped at the doorway to John's room surprised he wasn't in the Intensive Care Unit. Harold and a private nurse were there among all the machines that had lights blinking and soft noises emanating from them. John was in the bed with the head of it slightly elevated and he appeared to be sleeping.

The nurse quietly approached them. "I'm sorry, family only, no other visitors are allowed at this time to allow Mr. Hermanson to rest." She smiled at them.

"I decide who sees me." The low gruff voice came from the bed.

They all looked over at John surprised to hear his speak.

John opened both of his eyes and looked over at the nurse. "I asked for them to come. Why don't you take a break, about fifteen minutes worth?"

"But, Mr. Hermanson…"

Harold stepped over to the nurse and gently taking her by the elbow steered the nurse toward the door. "It will be fine, we won't upset him, I'll be here." Then he closed the door behind her. Turning around to face his dad, "Do you want me to leave also?"

"No, no, stay here. There have been too many secrets," his dad replied.

The two young people exchanged glances, "*Now what?*"

John spoke in a soft voice, "Come closer to the bed, I won't bite any of you. I'm just too tired to talk real loud."

When John saw they were where he wanted them he began. "I need to share something with you in case I have another episode. It was in this very room that your grandfather died, also of a heart attack and he said his last words to me, which were, 'Don't sell off any of my land or holdings when I'm gone, its business as usual. Nothing, understand? I have my reasons. Work with Jensen, he has my will. In the case that Jensen kicks the bucket and everything is status quo, find the secret drawer in my desk and follow my request. It's not notarized though, this (he tapped by his heart) happened. I repeat, don't sell anything. And John, I've loved you like a brother.' He took one last breath and he was gone." John stopped talking and looked Benjamin straight in the eyes, "And I do believe you are his grandson." Then he laid back and closed his eyes; they could see that this sharing had taken a lot out of him.

A knock on the door and the nurse entered. "Is everything okay?" She immediately walked over to access John and all the equipment around him.

Benjamin took John's hand, "Thank you, John. I'll come back tomorrow. You rest now."

John opened his eyes, "I'd like that, you too, JC."

"I will, John." JC patted his hand.

Harold was standing by the door and shook hands with Benjamin. "Thanks for coming. He needed to tell you that. I think he will rest comfortably now."

Holding hands, they walked down the corridor. Looking at her Benjamin asked, "The stairs or the elevator?"

"Um, if we take the stairs you might want to kiss me on each landing. Using the elevator and you might want to kiss me, but there might be someone else on it. Um, decisions, decisions." Her eyes were twinkling.

"In my humble opinion as an attorney, I say the stairs it is, just for the exercise factor, well maybe a reward at each floor." Benjamin held the door open for her.

"Counselor, good verdict," She smiled at him.

As they went down the stairs, JC questioned, "Benjamin? What is your opinion on what John said? Do you think you can find the secret drawer?" Stopping at the bottom of the steps and she pursed her lips. "The landing, remember? Kiss."

"Ah yes, must not forgo that in the quest for exercise." Benjamin leaned down and kissed her with much warmth.

The question went unanswered as laughing; she quickly started down the next flight of steps. History repeated itself and then they were on the ground floor.

"One for the road," Benjamin took her in his arms and in the middle of a nice embrace, the door opened and a doctor came rushing in. They jumped apart guilty as two teenagers.

The doctor just looked at them, remarked, "Carry on," and sprinted up the steps.

Laughing, they exited the building, "That will probably be all over the hospital before we reach the Jeep." JC commented looking at her watch, "I'd better get you home; I work tomorrow and need my beauty sleep."

"You are beautiful all the time." Benjamin's voice was serious as he opened the door of the vehicle.

Looking over at him, she started the Jeep. The look on his face said he meant it. The feeling of being special swept over her, and she smiled at him. "Thank you."

She was going to have some wonderful dreams tonight and it wouldn't be about some secret drawer. The drawer!

CHAPTER NINE

"Benjamin! Are you going to search for the secret drawer tonight?" Glancing at her wrist watch, "It's too late for me to be part of it tonight. Will you wait until tomorrow so I can help you? Please?" Her eyes were also pleading with him. "I know I really don't have any right to ask you, but I do love to solve a mystery."

Laughing, Benjamin snapped in his seat belt, "That must be why your family has been in the law enforcement work, always wanting to solve a mystery. Of course I will wait for you. I need to make contact with my office and take care of some correspondence. The drawer has been hidden for years; another day won't make any difference. Now put this Jeep into gear and take me home so you can get some rest. Tomorrow, bring a change of clothes, stop over after work and we will do some detective work on the desk."

"Thanks. It really isn't any of my business, but I am curious as what could possibly be in the drawer concerning the land that wouldn't have been in the will, knowing the drawer was secret enough that it might have never been found. Um. And to think for two years John knew something was concealed in the desk and never looked for it. He could have taken that information to his grave. Unbelievable." Turning into the lane, she came to a stop in front of the mansion, shifting the Jeep into park.

Unhooking the seat belt he turned slightly to face her. "I agree it's strange, but I think those two came from the old school where contracts were sealed with a hand- shake, a man's word meant something, and those two trusted each other implicitly." He leaned toward her, "Now, my little detective, how about a good night kiss to hold me over until tomorrow?"

* * *

Tim opened his eyes and moved slightly. He was stiff from being in that position so long. He rubbed his neck. *What was he doing sitting in the car?* Then he remembered and looked over to the empty spot where JC's jeep had been parked. In the light of a full moon, he could see it was gone. He hit his fist on the steering wheel, darn it, somehow he needed to convince her he was the man for her and get some money away from grandpa and dad.

Unscrewing the cap from the whiskey bottle, he took a gulp, and choked on the cheap whiskey. Opening the car door, he got out and relieved himself by the rear tire. Keeping a hand on the side of the car to steady himself, he slowly got back into the driver's seat.

With shaking hands, he took another drink, spilling some down the front of him. After a couple of tries, got the top back on the bottle, *time to go visit his woman.* He turned the key and the sound of the vehicle starting startled him. Putting the car in gear, he pushed his foot down with too much force causing the car to jerk forward crashing into a car in the next lane. Tim swore, slammed the car into reverse, and pulled around it. Nothing was going to stop him from seeing his JC.

Unbeknown to Tim, the whole incident was recorded on one of the security cameras in the parking lot. The hospital security officer who was operating the cameras debated with himself if he should call law enforcement or wait until tomorrow. He thought he could bring up the license plate, but his shift was almost over and he'd have to fill out forms. Wait and let whoever own the damaged car complain and the day shift could take care of it.

* * *

Something woke JC up. She rolled over in her bed and listened. She thought she heard noise by her front door. She was about to get out of bed when she saw a figure outside her bedroom window trying to open it. She glanced over at her gun; slowly slipped out of bed, grabbed her cell phone and jeans, keeping low, quietly crept into her living room and put a call through to headquarters with the code: possible break in. Slipping into her jeans, she grabbed her five-cell flashlight and eased out the back door to investigate. The grass was cold on her bare feet, but also made no noise as she quietly went around to the front of the house.

The man on the porch was so intently focused on trying to push open the window that wouldn't budge; he didn't hear or see JC approach him.

Turning the flashlight on in his face, she loudly ordered, "Put your hands in the air and turn around slowly."

Thoroughly surprised, the drunk stumbled as he turned and fell landing in a heap where JC had been standing.

She had quickly side stepped avoiding being knocked down.

"Stay put!" She commanded and put the full beam of the light on his face. "What the heck are you doing trying to break into my home, Tim?" As she leaned down to help him sit up she could smell the booze on him.

He grabbed her arm and pulled her on top of him. "I came to make love to you and show you I'm a better man than the city slicker." He tried to give her a kiss, but instead felt the full force of her fist into his face. "So, you want to play hard to get!" He swung back at her, but in his drunken condition, he missed and ended face down on the porch.

Quickly she put her knee into his back and twisting his arm up behind him applied pressure. "You better hold still if you ever want to use your drinking arm again."
"Ow, you're hurting me."

"Shut up, Tim and be still."

The crunch of tires in the driveway got JC's attention as the squad car stopped yards from her porch. They were investigating her call.

JC waved her free arm at them never releasing her hold on Tim, as they put on the search light.

"Having a party or a wrestling match, JC?"

"Funny, guys. Cuff him. It's Tim Hermanson. He had a little too much to drink, again. Book him on attempted breaking and entry with intent to assault. That was his words, he was going to show me what a man he is in the bedroom. I'll sign the complaint in the morning when I come in. Thanks for showing up so fast."

JC watched as the two officers loaded the swearing inebriated man into the backseat of the squad car. Then she quickly ran around to the back and went into the house, locking the door behind her. Her feet were freezing. Glancing at her clock, she groaned, 'only three more hours of sleep left'.

It seemed as if her head had just hit the pillow when the alarm clock went off. JC got ready for work. As she exited her front door, she noticed Tim's car about three car lengths down the street. As she drove by it, she noticed a lot of damage done to the front and side and made a mental note of it.

Arriving at work, she signed the complaint and noticed that Tim still had not contacted anyone. According to the report, he was too drunk and sleeping it off. She also noticed a hit and run report made by the hospital security. That could explain the damage she noticed on his vehicle. She shook her head. This wasn't the first time he damaged property because of drinking.

She glanced at her watch; she had time before she had to leave for her patrol route. JC took a chance that Harold would be home and gave him a call about Tim. He thanked her and said he would be in shortly before he went to the hospital to be with his dad.

When Harold arrived, JC ushered him into an office and explained what had transpired at her home. She also said that Tim's car had been in a hit and run accident in the hospital parking lot.

"Harold, I'm willing to drop my charges if we can get Tim to go into rehab for counseling. I can paint the window trim, and he didn't get to take advantage of me," she smiled at him, "Tim would have been sporting more than a sore arm today if he had tried. I can't speak for the party whose vehicle was damaged, but I think we should work out something where he has to do some labor to pay for the damages. I know you have paid insurance for him, but I'm sure you can think of something to impress him that unwise decisions lead to consequences. I know John could." JC chuckled, "I bet John would figure out how many hours of mucking out stalls, doing some hand weeding etc it would take to pay off that amount."

"I'm really sorry, JC. I don't know what has gotten into him. He wasn't always this way." Harold shook his head.

"I think the judge will make a thirty day inpatient for alcohol rehab mandatory and would take our suggestion into consideration on the work program. You would pay him the same amount as any hired hand and on payday, he would turn that money into the judge until reimbursement was met. Or, the judge just might have some other type of work so as not to make you the heavy on this."

"I appreciate your recommendation in this manner. Here are the two of you, both the same age, you are such a wonderful productive lady, and he is so indolent." Harold took a deep sigh. "Where did his mother and I go wrong?"

Putting her hand on his arm, she replied, "If I had the answers to that, I'd have the best seller. I think it is normal to give kids the best we can, and maybe make it too easy. I also think that he might be prone to use alcohol as a crutch. Let's see if we can't make this a positive turning point in his life. I'll send a note over to the judge; you get a lawyer for Tim and let's hope for the best."

Harold stood up and extended his hand to JC. After they shook hands, he raised up his arms, "And now a hug for our little girl, you always have been part of our family too."

Tears welled up in her eyes. "Yeah, you always were like a special uncle to me. Say hi to John. Benjamin and I will be over to see him later."

Watching Harold leave the office with his head down and shoulders drooping, JC hoped this all worked, she didn't want to see Tim waste his life and become another Jake. She shook her head sadly, *what was the magic solution to make Tim change his ways?*

CHAPTER TEN

Benjamin sat on the porch swing watching for JC. *He missed her bright smile and the way she made him feel when she was around: content, special, family. Family? Um, where did that word come from? No other woman had ever made him feel this way. He was surprised at how fast the attraction for each other had occurred. He felt like a school boy sometimes around her instead of a respected attorney.*

He stopped the swing with his foot when her Jeep made the turn into the lane. He stood up and went down the steps as the Jeep came to a stop.

Going around to the driver's side he opened the door. "Good afternoon. I missed you."

Laughing as she exited the Jeep, "And I missed you," she reached up her arms around his neck.

Benjamin bent his head down and they shared a warm kiss. And then another.

Looking up at him, JC smiled, "That was a nice welcome."

"My pleasure." Benjamin gave her a hug. "Well, my lady, are you ready to go hunting for a secret drawer?"

"Can we let it wait for a bit? I'll tell you while we go to see John. You will never believe happened last night after I went to bed."

"No problem, John is a good man and who knows; he might know where the secret drawer is and tell us how to find it." Benjamin hugged her and gave her a kiss on the nose, "I'll just go lock the door."

JC got back into the driver's seat as Benjamin took the steps two at a time and secured the door.

Benjamin returned to the car and on their way to the hospital, JC related Tim's attempt to break in and his arrest.

Benjamin had remained silent as she talked. He wasn't so sure that this was just a drunk trying to seduce her.

"Has he tried getting fresh with you before?" Benjamin's' voice was quiet and the tone was similar to what he would use with a young person on the witness stand.

"Oh, he has asked me out a few times, but honestly, even if he wasn't lazy and drinks too much, he isn't my type. There is no spark there between us and I've known him all my life." Stopping at the stop sign, she did a quick side glance over at Benjamin and taking her hand off the wheel, touched his arm, "Now you, you give me a spark."

Benjamin took her hand in his and kissed it then releasing it so she had both hands on the wheel. *Spark? He was feeling more of a lightning jolt.* "You described my feelings exactly."

JC blushed as she pulled away from the stop sign, *now why did she say that? Maybe because no man had ever made her feel like this before, special! These feeling were happening way to fast. Oh I wish I had a woman to talk with about this!* Taking a deep breath she changed the subject, "When I talked with Harold this morning about Tim, I said we would stop in and see John this afternoon. He said John would like that. John has been a big part of my life."

They were both silent in their thoughts for a moment and then JC spoke, "I'm sorry for dominating our discussion, how did your day go?"

"I had a conference call with the office to decide what cases we will take. Some can involve months and I really don't want to go back right now." He squeezed her gently on the shoulder. "Work was always my passion, but every time I look over the pending cases, all I see is your lovely face. Is there a solution for this?"

"A ha. I think there is." Pulling into the parking lot and shutting off the motor, she released her seat belt and leaned over to Ben kissing him passionately on the lips. As she moved to get closer her elbow hit the horn button and they both jumped and began laughing defusing the amorous moment.

"I think we better go see John." She smoothed her long blond hair back and reached for the door handle, "And I'll see what I can think of for a solution to your problem." She had a beguiling smile on her face.

* * *

Looking down from John's window, Harold turned to his dad, "I think JC and Benjamin are sweet on each other."

Chuckling, John responded, "Willard would have loved that." He rubbed his hands together, "The ole love bug sometimes bites pretty fast. Your ma and I never spent a long time a courtin. We knew our own mind."

Harold watched as the two held hands and walked toward the hospital. "I guess I shouldn't get caught watching them. He brought a chair closer to his dad and then poured some fresh water into John's empty glass. Putting the container back on the table, he sat down by John, "So, what did Dr. Greenwood say about you today?"

"Ah he is still yapping about getting that by pass done. I feel pretty good now; I don't see why I can't wait awhile longer." John took a sip of his water.

From the doorway came the reply, "Because John, we want you around for a long time, healthy and overseeing everything, not flying around in angel wings." JC came over and hugged him. "So, why not let Harold set up the time with Dr. Greenwood? Make a new man out of you, one that doesn't get out of breath or pass out on us." She kissed the top of his head and then went and sat on the foot of his bed.

"They have some pretty slick new procedures that make this a piece of cake, not like it used to be, where you were an invalid for a month or three." Benjamin added. "Why you could convalesce on my front porch being waited on hand and foot and watch the traffic out front and Harold would give you the low down on what is going on with the farms and animals."

John gave him a pensive look, "And what are you going to be doing, high tailing it back to the big city are yah?"

Benjamin sat down next to JC and put his arm around her shoulders, "I'm getting really attached to all of you around here. Just as you can keep your thumb on business, I can do a lot of it via the computer and phone with mine in New York. I can fly in and back again the same day if need be. By looking over granddad's business dealings, he did a lot from right here in Freedomville."

At that moment, John's private nurse returned from her break and seeing the couple sitting on her patient's bed was upset. "What are you doing sitting on Mr. Hermanson's bed. Are you trying to put germs there?"

"No, Missy, they were tuckered out since they just convinced me to have that confounded bi-pass thingy done. So simmer down and go put that bug in the doc's ear to get things in motion." John waved his hand dismissing her.

Surprised and pleased she quickly exited the room to spread the news to Dr. Greenwood. She didn't know how they did it, but they must have some magic charm to get that grouchy old man to consent to the needed surgery.

"John, could you tell us where the secret drawer is in the desk?" JC asked.

"You mean you two haven't found it yet?" John laughed.

"We haven't had a chance to look for it." Benjamin responded.

Old John looked over at Harold and spoke as if JC and Benjamin weren't there, "Maybe they are spending too much time getting to know each other, a little snuggling maybe." His eyes were twinkling as he saw the two blush, but they not deny his reasoning.

Then John got serious, "As you sit down in the chair, on the right side above the top drawer there is a board that pulls out, like a cutting board in the kitchen cupboards. Pull it out as far as it will go. Now, take the drawer in front of you and pull that completely out of the desk. There are two buttons on the right side of the wall of the desk. Press them both at the same time and the board can now be pulled completely out. The end has a keyhole that can be opened by the same key that locks the desk up. I have no idea what Willard had in there or why he didn't tell Jensen in case I kicked the bucket." John leaned back, tired. "Maybe he was tuckered out too, but I would like to see what you find out…if you want to share that is. It may be nothing, who knows, but your granddad wasn't a jokester, he always meant what he said."

"You look tired, John, I think it is time for us to go and check out that desk. Harold, want to walk down with us?" JC gave Harold a look of 'don't say no'.

"Sure, I'll be right back Dad. If I see the nurse, I'll tell her you need some fresh water.

JC gave John a hug and Benjamin shook his hand. "See you tomorrow, John, rest well."

Walking down the corridor, they paused by the waiting room. Seeing no one in there they took a seat.

"Harold, I didn't want to say anything in front of John not knowing if you told him about last night or not. How did it go with Tim today?"

"He is still sitting in jail. I refused to post bond for him. It's time for some, what do they call it, 'tough love'? The court date is a two days from today. I sure hope Dad has his surgery tomorrow and is better so I can be there. I can't be at both places at the same time." Harold shook his head.

Benjamin spoke up "I applaud your actions, Harold. I know it is hard to take this route, but hopefully this will wake your son up. I've handled cases when it was worse and all the money parents have spent and then finally something happens, a life is lost and then the remorse sets in and I hear, 'if I only had...' you fill in the words."

"Thanks you two. I better get back up to dad and make sure he doesn't change his mind about the surgery." Harold waved and retraced his steps to his dad's room.

CHAPTER ELEVEN

The young couple stood hand and hand looking at the huge desk.

"Did you ever pull out that wooden tray or board and use it to put files on or anything?" She asked Benjamin as she went to sit in the chair in front of the desk.

"No, when I was going through the files from the safe, the desk is so large that I didn't need to use it." He sat down on the comfy old desk chair and ran his hands over the desk. "Such a beautiful desk: I never would have thought to look for a secret compartment if he hadn't mentioned it."

After removing the key chain from his pocket, he inserted the one for the desk. Looking up at JC, "Aren't you coming over on this side to help?" He smiled as she quickly joined him.

He pulled the middle desk drawer all the way out, and placed it on the desk top. Then he knelt down and found the two buttons on the side. Looking up at her he asked, "Ready? I'm going to push on them now." He lightly pressed on them and they both heard the click as it released the board. "Pull it out all the way."

With the shelf on the desk so the key hole was available, JC asked him, "Are you ready for the mystery hiding inside?"

Nodding his head in the affirmative, Benjamin inserted the key and gently turned it. They both heard the click. She laid the tray down flat and Benjamin pressed lightly on the end and it eased open enough for him to pull it out. The tension was thick in the room as he removed a thin number ten envelope.

Written in a bold strong cursive in the middle of the envelope was Benjamin's name.

"I wonder when granddad put this in here. Why didn't Mr. Jensen or John say something earlier about it?" Benjamin looked over at JC. "Would you think it weird if I told you I have mixed feelings about opening this?"

She shook her head no. "Would you like me to leave so you can go through it alone?"

"No, no, somehow I feel you should be in on this with me. What if John had died and not told me about this? I wonder if there is something else in the old safe that I haven't gotten to that would have told me about it." Benjamin slid the drawer back in and sat down in the chair. "Slide your chair closer by me so we can read it together."

Lifting the unsealed flap he removed three sheets of single spaced typed papers. There were pictures of him, his dad and mom and the law firm they owned.

Tears wet Benjamin's eyes as he looked at his parents. He ran his fingers over it. He missed them. He handed the pictures to JC so she go inspect them closer.

"Oh my gosh. You look just like your dad and grandpa. It's uncanny how you all look like brothers." She kept looking between Benjamin and the photographs.

Choked with emotion, Benjamin just nodded and picked up the papers. At the top of the first page was the date of the month his grandfather passed away.

"My Dear Benjamin,

Hopefully you find this secret compartment or John will reveal it to you. I didn't put what is in this letter into the will, I should have, but in my old age, I am hoping you will find this and do right by my wishes.

I have secretly known where you three have been and how you were doing. I had a private detective firm on a retainer ever since I finally had a return city to look for him. I never told your grandmother that William survived; I thought not being able to see him was worse than thinking he had drowned. I regret that now. We should have brought him home and those that didn't believe his version of the accident, well too bad. But I respected his wishes.

From afar, I watched as William and then you progressed and became good, honest attorneys. I actually was behind the scenes when your dad was securing some of the loans he got from the bank when he opened his first office and then purchased the building you are in now. I owned that bank. I was the silent partner so to speak.

Recently I found out from the doctor that I don't have much time left. It was all I could do not to call you, but I didn't have the energy to deal with all the emotion at this time. And I had Janice Caroline here. How I love that young woman. She is like my own child and has made her grandparents and me very proud of her.

You noticed that there was to be a two year delay from the time I pass until Jensen was to get in touch with you. That was so he could observe how you managed your affairs and remained the upright person you were. If you didn't, you would have never known about me."

Benjamin looked over at JC, laid down the sheet and picked up the next one and continued reading it out loud.

"You wouldn't have known about me because everything I owned would have gone to Janice Caroline."

JC's head jerked up and she looked over at Benjamin. "Oh my goodness! This is the first time I've heard about this. Honest! In his will he paid off the mortgage of my home and my Jeep. No one knew anything else that was in the will and the farms went on as usual. Every so often a donation to the community would be made in your grandfather's name and we thought that was probably something he had set up in his will." JC jumped up and walked around the desk visibly upset. "This is crazy! Why didn't Jensen say something?"

Benjamin quickly got up, went around the desk and put his arm around her, "I believe you. Who knows what was going on in his mind? He was getting on in years and had a heart condition. I could see him giving you all of it, really. He loved you dearly and he personally had never met me." He gave her a kiss on the cheek, "Let's see what else he has to say." He led her back to her chair, sat back in his and resumed reading the letter out loud.

"I worked hard to acquire what I have. I believe one should share with those less fortunate and have done so all of my life. Your grandmother and I were God fearing people. We didn't let people know where some of their 'good luck' came from. Other times we did such things as pay for the wing of the hospital or stained glass windows for the church. I hope you will continue in this way as I know Janice Caroline would. As the scriptures say, 'Of those who have much, much is required.'

Everyone that worked for me has been provided for. It is my wish that they continue in their jobs until they no longer are able. A person who has something to do is a happier person.

Now, here is the gist of this letter, Mr. Jensen has all the deeds to the properties and as you know there was a portion of the will he didn't reveal to you. He told you all in due time per my instructions.

This is it. IF you decide to sell off any of the property, then JC inherits the mansion and the farm surrounding it and everything in or on said property. She has loved this place, and it was a second home to her. It shouldn't go to strangers. There is plenty of other property and you have the wealth that you and your father accumulated."

Benjamin placed the sheet of paper on top of the other one and looked at JC.

Tears were running down her face. She wiped them off with her sleeve, and with a choked up voice, "I swear I didn't know anything about this."

Benjamin patted her arm and picked up the last sheet. "And no one else, evidently."

"I should say too, that she was such a blessing to my dear Elizabeth and she has been here constantly for me too, being hostess for many occasions at the mansion and being with me now as my time grows short. I haven't told her how serious my condition is, but she is here all the time giving me comfort. I love her dearly.

My prayer is that the two of you will be friends and you will always treat her as someone special.

I have loved you from away, and wish I had come forward so we could have been the family we should have been. I didn't care what the community would have thought, but I had to respect your father's wishes he so asked for those many years ago.

Peace be with you,
Your grandfather,
Willard Murphy"

The signature was in the same bold handwriting that was on the front of the envelope.

JC and Benjamin looked at each other and sat there in silence, each contemplating what he had just read. This was a lot to digest.

CHAPTER TWELVE

JC drove home in a daze. *The mansion could be hers if Benjamin wanted to sell any of it. Not only could the lovely mansion be hers, but the farm around it.* She shook her head. This must be a dream. She turned into her driveway and shut off the Jeep.

Taking off her seatbelt she continued to sit there thinking. *I basically own the mansion with all of its beautiful antique furniture; all the history located in the attic and memories, all the memories of the fun and love in the home that I grew up in. Mine that is, if Benjamin ever wants to sell off any of the land.*

She hit her fist against the steering wheel with frustration. This was so confusing. Would he sell? What if he never sold anything? She shook her head. I feel like I was just handed a present but told not to open it.

JC got out of the Jeep and with a burst of temper slammed the door shut. *In those last days when Willard lay dying, holding on to my hand, I tended to his every need, day and night because I loved him, except for when skilled nursing was necessary and he never even whispered a word about any this. Nothing. Not one word about knowing his son had survived the accident, that he had a grandson but would leave everything to her IF Mr. Jensen deemed Benjamin was less than perfect. What on earth would constitute 'less than perfect' in Jensen's opinion? Would a parking ticket or cheating on his income tax qualify?*

Frustrated she bent down, picked up a rock from the driveway and hurled it as far as she could, then began to cry. *So, Willard had known all these years about everything and kept it all to himself! This wasn't fair. Why even let her know, when everything revolved over what Benjamin would do? To raise up her hopes knowing how much she loved the mansion, wasn't right. It had been a second home to her. Then to dangle the possibility that it could be hers wasn't ethical to her.* Sniffing she wiped her tears with the back of her hand.

In a dejected slouch, she slowly walked toward the house, then stopped abruptly.

Benjamin. Was this really the first time he knew about the letter? Had he found the secret letter before? Was it really possible Mr. Jensen or old John wasn't privy to all of this? What about the safe? Was there a note somewhere in there about this?

Could this be a joke? Or was Willard trying to be a match maker between her and Benjamin to keep the wealth in the 'family' so to speak. She needed to talk with Mr. Jensen.

* * *

Benjamin stayed on the porch until the tail lights of the Jeep disappeared from his view. He leaned against the pillar going over in his mind what had transpired.

It bothered him how upset JC was with the information in his grandfather's letter. He shook his head. Jensen had to know something about this...tomorrow they were going to have a discussion. As an attorney, he knew this should never have been allowed.

Would JC think he knew about this letter and was faking his affection for her to keep her in the dark or basically steal from her? Doesn't she know how much I care for her?

Pushing away from the post, he went inside to re-read the letter. Maybe it would make more sense the second time.

* * *

"Mr. Murphy, I know you are upset, but you of all people understand about confidentiality as much as I do. No laws were broken. I did as your grandfather instructed." Mr. Jensen stood up, placing his hands on the desk, spreading his fingers out, "Your grandfather wasn't the usual client. He had a mind of his own. I did what he asked me to, as his attorney and also as a friend. He was so lonely after your grandmother died and waited anxiously for each report from the investigators about you and your dad. You could say he lived for those reports." Jensen dropped heavily back into his chair.

"Why didn't he have all of this detailed in the will? This was your responsibility as his lawyer to have all the ends taken care of. Was he becoming senile? Where's the rest of the will? Why were you told to wait two years before contacting me? If I wasn't whatever grandfather thought I should be, you would have automatically given everything to JC. She really should have been given that anyway. For someone who was treated like a granddaughter she deserved more than a Jeep and her mortgage paid off. That wouldn't have bothered me. I have more than enough and she deserved it."

Benjamin stood up and ran his hand through his hair, then turned around to face Mr. Jensen, "You realize that this letter of his wasn't notarized and there were no signatures of any witnesses. It is just his wishes. If I wanted to I could legally ignore his letter. I won't, but if there are any other surprises in store for me, I want to know about them now."

Not saying a word, Mr. Jensen walked over to the wall cabinet, punched in a code to open the door. Retrieving a brown organizer, he returned to his desk. Sliding the thick folder over to Benjamin, "This is the total of your inheritance."

Taking a deep breath, Benjamin picked it up and walked over to the window. Flipping open the portfolio he quickly perused it. Then he slowly sat back down in the chair.

"Well?" asked Mr. Jensen.

"All of this? No strings attached?" Benjamin said quietly.

"No strings free and clear. Your grandfather had a canny knowledge of investments. I've had an accounting firm taking care of all of these accounts." Mr. Jensen had a smug look on his face and he retrieved a card from his desk drawer and handed it to Benjamin. "They are waiting for your call to take control of these assets."

Benjamin was silent for a minute absorbing what he has just been told. He had just gone from a very wealthy man to owning billions. For some odd reason a line in one of the letters his grandfather had written came to him that was also part of a scripture from Luke 12:48, "For unto whomsoever much is given, of him shall be much required." It spoke to him as an image of JC's tear covered face floated in his mind.

Thoughtfully he raised his head and quietly but firmly said to Mr. Jensen, "I want you to draw up a deed for the mansion and the farm surrounding it."

Jensen straightened up, his face turning red with frustration, "You can't sell that property, per the will!" He slammed his hand down on the paper work.

Very calmly, Benjamin replied, "Excuse me; this wasn't a codicil to the will. This was an old man's last wishes that made no sense at all. Legally, I don't have to do anything it says. You know it and I know it. Besides, I'm not selling it, I'm deeding it or should I say gifting it over to JC. It has memories for her that I will never have. It will also provide her with income for years. All I want from the mansion is a picture of the family I never knew."

Jensen shook his head, "You need to take some time and think this over. Do you realize the value of the mansion and the land, not to mention the antiques? I know how much Willard loved JC, but to break up the land…" Jensen was disturbed over this, but he knew by the look on Benjamin's face, nothing would deter him. He sighed, once more in control of his emotions. "I can have it ready by tomorrow afternoon. Are you sure about this Benjamin? This is the family home, part of your history. You need to take more time to think this over. At least sleep on it over night. It's part of your inheritance, your roots!" In all the years Mr. Jensen had been an attorney, he had never had someone give away a fortune like this.

His face composed, Benjamin replied, "You don't understand. I have feelings for JC that I've never felt for anyone before. I seriously think you could say I've fallen in love with her. I don't want her to think I'm being nice to her because of the mansion. I want it to be hers with no strings attached, not wondering if or when it might be hers. Do you understand? You weren't there when we read that letter and I could tell she was deeply hurt. Shocked could be an apt word. My heart ached for her."

Jensen nodded his head. "You have a lot of your granddad in you. I'll have it ready for you to read. If it has your approval, you can sign it. When do you want JC to know about it?"

"I'll take care of that. See you tomorrow." Benjamin leaned over the desk to shake the man's hand. "Tomorrow afternoon."

* * *

Mr. Jensen worked JC in at two in the afternoon so she and Benjamin wouldn't meet when he picked up the deed to the mansion and farm. She wasn't happy to have to wait until then but Jensen wouldn't discuss any of it over the phone. As he expected, she was emotional when she arrived.

"But Mr. Jensen, this doesn't make any sense to me." Agitated, JC got up from her chair and marched over to stand looking out the window, her arms crossed in front of her. "Why didn't Willard say anything to me, especially when he was dying? Are you sure Benjamin didn't know anything about this until we located it last night?"

"Come sit down, JC. Let's go over this calmly." Mr. Jensen took her gently by the elbow and escorted her back to the chair in front of his desk. "Would you like some coffee or water?"

JC shook her head no. "This is like a carrot being dangled in front of a mule. I love that mansion. It was my second home. I know every nook and cranny of it and enjoyed being the princess of the castle when I was a little girl. Now!" She stood up again, unable to harness her emotions, "If Benjamin sells any of the property, then the mansion is mine, if he doesn't, I can just wish or dream about it. It doesn't make any sense at all." JC slumped down into the chair. "He could let it crumble into ruin. What's to prevent him from firing everyone and going back to New York?"

"Do you really think Benjamin is that type of man, JC?" Mr. Jensen said the words softly, leaning back into his chair, his fingers pressed together in a tent fashion. "Do you realize this was just the wishes of a dying man? It isn't a legal document. Benjamin doesn't have to honor it."

JC was silent for a few minutes and Mr. Jensen didn't say anything to interrupt her thoughts.

Looking up at Mr. Jensen, JC whispered, "It's not legal?"

"No it's not. There was nothing attached to the will either. You really have no claim on the wishes of an dying man."

JC sighed, "I suppose it's no secret that I'm crazy about Benjamin. I know it's foolish to be swept away like I have been. I'm the granddaughter of a sheriff, a police officer. I'm trained to do a fast assessment of a person, and at no time have

I felt Benjamin is underhanded. From the first time I met him, I felt a connection with him. I care for him deeply."

The last sentence came out so quietly, Mr. Jensen almost didn't hear it.

"JC, did Benjamin mention finding anything in the safe concerning this letter?"

She straightened up. "You know, he did mention that he needed to go through the safe and wondered if there would be something in there to tell about the secret drawer since it didn't say anything in the will. What if old John had passed away, the letter might never have been found. I guess it doesn't matter anyway, it wasn't a legal document. Benjamin can do whatever he wants to. It's all his."

The phone ringing interrupted them. "Yes, she is here. One moment please." Mr. Jensen handed the receiver to JC, "The clerk from the court house is on the phone."

"Officer Smith, speaking."

"Hi, JC. The judge wants you in court since you were the arresting officer of Tim Hermanson. Can you come over right away?"

"No one told me to be there today. I'll be right there, give me five minutes." JC leaned across the desk and hung up the phone. "Duty calls. Too bad I'm not working today so I would get paid." She smiled and rose from the chair.

"Forget that I was here and my outburst. What will be, will be. I have a comfortable home and life and as grandpa would have said, "Little girl, be contented with what you have, because some aren't as fortunate." She gave a slight wave at Mr. Jensen, "Duty calls. Bye." She swiftly left the room.

In some ways, she felt relieved not to have the mansion between her and Benjamin, always wondering if it would ever be hers.

* * *

The judge looked over at Tim sitting in the witness stand. "Tim, I've known you since you were a baby. You come from good hard working people and for that reason we have left some of your misbehavior slide by. Your grandfather or dad has bailed you out numerous times. You have finally worn out their patience and mine, and it is time you grow up and face the consequences of your actions.

Do you realize how destructive your life has been the last five years? You are spiraling down a deep hole, but you still have time to straighten up and be an example of the heritage your family has been to each other and the community.

For attempting to break into Janice Caroline Smith's home to molest her, you are sentenced for thirty days in jail to be served after the month in rehab for your alcoholism. We also have proof that your car was involved in a hit and run in the hospital parking lot. I have here three estimates on the cost of repairs. You are going to work off that amount after your thirty days in jail. I have made contact with Pastor Haroldson who needs some painting done on the parish house, the garage, the church basement and the utility shed. I have spoken with a professional painter and he has given me the cost of doing these jobs and that would also be the amount to repair the damage to the vehicle you hit in the hospital parking lot and your fine for drunk and disorderly conduct. You are also ordered to stay away from Janice Smith's property until I rescind the order."

The judge looked over at JC. "Officer Smith, please approach the bench."

She waited while they opened the gate to let her stand before the desk. Looking over at Tim who sat hunched in his chair, her heart ached to see how disheveled he was.

"Are you satisfied with my ruling, JC?" The judge peered down over his glasses at her.

"Yes, your, Honor. Tim comes from a long line of productive people, and I think once he realizes what control alcohol has over him, he will be the man he wants to be."

Tim jumped up jabbing his finger in the air at her, shouted, "It's all your fault! I drink because you won't give me the time of day. I love you and you only have eyes for that stranger."

The court officer put his hand on Tim's arm, "Sit down."

Tim plopped back into his chair bursting into tears.

JC went to him and touched his arm. "Tim, we played together as kids, but I don't love you as a woman. You need help to overcome your dependency of alcohol and you will see the world open up to you."

Never saying a word or acknowledging she said anything, he jerked his arm away from her and kept his head down.

JC step back, nodded to the judge and returned to her seat in the court room. *Why did life have to be so complicated?*

As the judge left the courtroom, she felt her phone vibrating in her pocket. Checking it she saw it was from Harold. She had wondered why he hadn't been in court for Tim.

"Hello, Harold."

"JC, can you come over to the hospital? Dad came through the surgery just fine for his age, but keeps saying your name. I think if you were here he would relax."

"I'll be right there. The judge just gave the sentence on Tim; I think he is still feeling the effects of the alcohol and doesn't really comprehend all of it yet."

Harold's sigh carried over the phone. "I couldn't be two places at once and I felt I had to be here for dad. I'm so sorry to put you through all of this, JC."

"No problem, Harold. I'm leaving the court house as we speak and should be there shortly." JC shut off the phone and quickly went to her Jeep.

CHAPTER THIRTEEN

Walking into John's room JC was surprised to see Benjamin occupying one of the chairs next to the bed. Harold was in the other.

Both men stood up as she went to the foot of John's bed. The machines were making colored lines and beeps, tubes went from them to John's body. He laid there with his eyes closed, his winkled face almost as white as the sheets on his bed. John was an elderly man now and this surgery had taken a toll on him.

Slowly she made way alongside the bed until she could touch the hand that didn't have needles attached some place. "John, it's JC, I'm here."

John's eyes fluttered and then he focused on her. "Go with your heart, it will be okay." His voice was soft and hoarse from the tube that had been through his nose and down into his stomach. Then he closed his eyes and went into a peaceful sleep.

JC raised her eyes to meet Benjamin's. She saw warmth and love there.

Feeling the comfort of Harold's arm around her shoulders, she leaned her head on his chest. That felt so good to feel his strength. "Let's step out into the hall," he whispered, and with his arm still around her shoulders, let the way out of the room and down to the waiting room.

Benjamin, seeing that John was asleep, followed them.

Harold seated JC, and then took a chair next to her.

Benjamin filled two cups of coffee, handed one to each of them, and then got one for himself and sat close next to JC.

She looked over at him, smiled, "Thanks, I needed this, it has been an exhausting day. How did the surgery go, Harold?"

"It went better than we expected. However, I have to tell you before he went in, Benjamin came over to be with us. Dad asked him what he found in the secret drawer, and," Harold looked over at Benjamin, "Benjamin told us what it said. It was quite a surprise. Dad asked him what he was going to do, and Benjamin told him. Dad was content with the answer. Now, fill me in on the trial."

JC looked back and forth at the two men, she really wanted to know what Benjamin said, but whatever it was satisfied John and she was reassured with his message to her.

She related the sentence the judge had given Tim and about Tim's outburst. "You realize, Harold that Tim is an alcoholic. Thankfully, the judge did take into consideration my recommendation I suggested earlier when we talked with the rehab and working off the damages and fine. The judge could have thrown the book at Tim because of his multiple past run in with the law. Sometimes, I think the promise of an inheritance instead of working for your money is bad for kids." JC smiled, "What do I know; I don't have any kids or any inheritance to leave them if I did. Oh, and I need to visit with the pastor and thank him for his cooperation, he could have said no when I approached him about having Tim do the painting."

JC stood up and the men did too. She hugged Harold and then turned to Benjamin who had his arms open. She stepped into them and felt the warmth of his arms gently close around her. It wasn't his fault for his grandfather's odd way of doing things.

"Would you like to go out for dinner tonight, or we could eat in at the mansion. I think we need to talk. You were very upset last night when you left and I didn't know what to say. In this short time we've known each other I think we both realize that there is something between us besides my grandfather." Benjamin's eyes pleaded with her to say, yes."

Her eyes told him she felt that way too. There was a lot to discuss. To lighten up the emotion in the room, JC cocked her head to the right and then the left, "Um, decisions, decisions. Dress up, or jeans and a pizza."

Benjamin smiled at her, "I have another idea, could you get off for the next three days and fly with me to New York. We could have dinner on the way if you can leave tonight. Just pack an overnight bag, something to wear tomorrow, and I'll take you on a shopping spree after I ask Betty of the best places to go. I want you to see where I live and work. It will give you a break from all the stress you have been through lately." Getting excited about the possibility of her going to New York with him he added, "I bet I can even get some tickets for a play and you can really dress up." Then he got serious, "Plus, I need to personally attend to some things at the office."

"I, I've never been to New York. It sounds like fun. Let me call the captain and see if I can get the time off. I certainly have vacation days I haven't used."

With laughter in Harold's eyes, he rubbed his hands together, "Well, that sounds like a fun time, except for the shopping part, I hate to shop. I'm going back by dad, you two have a great time and I'll want a souvenir when you get back." He laughed and left the room.

* * *

"How were you ever able to get a plane this fast?" JC questioned as the sign came on that they could unbuckle their seat belts.

"It's mine, or I should say the companies. I called and had the pilots bring it here this afternoon. Either today or tomorrow, I needed to return to New York for a few cases they need some help with. I was keeping my fingers crossed that you would say yes to coming with me." Benjamin took her hand and gave it a gentle squeeze. "I want you to see the other side of me, the suits, the head of a firm, the lawyer."

The stewardess stopped by them, "Would you like dinner now, Mr. Murphy?"

"Why yes, Colleen, that would be fine. I'm hungry."

"Me too, I'm famished, it's been a long time since breakfast," JC chimed in.

The trip was uneventful, for which JC was grateful and she was surprised when they stepped off the plane to be met with a limousine waiting for them.

The police officer from the little town of Freedomville had a hard time concealing the little girl in her with the drive through New York to the condominium where Benjamin lived. The huge buildings, the busy traffic, the sidewalks packed with people. She was asking questions left and right. When they got to his building, a door attendant opened the limo door and another person took their luggage to the elevator that went to his floor! He lived on the entire sixth floor!

As Benjamin unlocked the door, a slim, elderly attractive woman approached them. She was dressed in dark blue slacks and a light blue top with long sleeves. A multi colored scarf was artfully draped around her neck. She wore a small pair of opal earrings in her ears. Her long hair with streaks of gray running through it was arranged on top of her head. JC wondered who she was and why she was there.

"JC, I want you to meet, Betty. Betty, this is Janice Caroline Smith from Freedomville where I own some property. Betty has been with the family for years and I couldn't get along without her. She oversees the firm when I'm gone, arranges everything in my private life, parties that are held here and supervises the cleaning staff. There is a maid's quarter where she stays if I have overnight guests or anything else is needed. If you have any questions or want anything, this is the lady to go to."

"Miss Smith, follow me and I'll show you to your room." She looked over at Benjamin and then down at the single suitcase, "Is that all the luggage?"

"Yes, Betty. Tomorrow I need you to make a list of places I can take JC to go shopping. You have such good taste in clothes." Benjamin replied.

"Thank you my dear for saying that." Betty nodded her head acknowledging his compliment. "There are a lot of boutiques to choose from in this large city."

"You are staying the night, aren't you, Betty?" Benjamin asked as he picked up his heavy suitcase. "I don't want the New York Times having a story about JC being here alone with me. Hopefully we will keep the gossips with no material."

"Of course, Benjie. What time would you like breakfast?"

Benjamin looked at JC, "Would you like to go to the office with me in the morning, I'll be back about 11:00 and we can have an early lunch and then I'll take you shopping."

"I'll stay here and look around. I really didn't bring clothes for the office. You told me to travel light." JC laughed.

"Betty, I'll have breakfast at seven then and have my car brought around by 7:30."

"JC, let Betty get you settled in while I check my messages and I'll join you in the study." Benjamin left the entryway for his room.

"This way, Miss Smith," Betty said as she picked up JC's suitcase. *It would be nice to observe this woman Bengie brought home.*

"Call me JC, Betty. Back home, I'm JC or Officer Smith. Only the young ones call me Miss Smith." JC smiled and followed her.

As Betty led the way she thought, *It's so refreshing to see a young woman not putting on airs. She is so different from the others trying to snag Bengie.*

* * *

Betty left the room, softly closing the door behind her.

Slowly JC turned around and leaned back against the door taking in her room. Room! It was almost as big as her home in Freedomville. She was standing in what could be called a sitting room or living room with huge windows looking out on the busy New York section of town. The furniture sure wasn't purchased from one of the box stores. Over to one side was a desk with a computer and printer for guests to use. There were live plants artfully arranged throughout the room giving a home like feeling. The pictures on the walls were vivid with color and unusual frames making the room seem alive. The walls were a pale green color. She was surprised it wasn't the dark colors so in vogue now.

Walking into the bedroom, she was surprised to find the king size bed didn't dominate the room.

Here the cream-colored walls were filled with outstanding pictures of landscapes and animals. Looking closely, she didn't recognize any of the artist's names. Bookcases filled with a variety reading material with a lounge chair and table placed close to them.

Through another open door was a dressing room where Betty had placed her suitcase. There was closet space for clothes and extra toiletries if needed. One wall was all mirror. Oh my gosh, this room was the size of her bedroom at home. She shook her head, unbelievable.

Advancing to the bathroom, JC thought it resembled an ad for the most expensive bathroom fixtures. The main color was blue with various shades except for the glass shower. There was a separate tub, plus a small hot tub. Unlit candles were placed around the tub. Soft thick towels and washcloths were stacked on glass shelves. There were also cotton robes of various sizes. She shook her head, wow, this sure beat Motel Six.

Going back to the bedroom, she put her brown oversized leather handbag on the dresser, removed her gun and badge from her leg holster and was placing them in the top drawer of the nightstand, when she noticed the large bouquet of fresh flowers had an envelope leaning against the vase with her name printed on it. Opening the envelope, she pulled out the card. "Welcome to my home, JC. You're more beautiful than any flowers. Be comfortable. Love, Benjamin."

She smiled and she wondered when he had time to order these. Everything happened so fast back home; they were together except when she went to pack a suitcase.

Taking a deep breath of the flower fragrance, she left to find the study where Benjamin would be.

Walking slowly down the hallway gave her the impression of being in an art museum with the busts and small statues on pedestals. She was absorbing it all when she heard Benjamin's voice and went in that direction. She stopped at the doorway.

"You better have another talk with your client to keep his emotions under control. You and I realize that the mother of his children is mentally unstable, but he won't get full custody with those outbursts when she lies on the stand. Get some food in him; have him lay off the coffee and donuts and if need be, he might need to see his doctor for a mild sedative so he can sleep at night. He is totally worn out with the ex-wife's actions, the upset kids and money issues. I didn't see in your notes where you have brought up the fact of how she emptied the bank accounts and all. Have those documents witnessed by the bank and you need two more opinions from the health professionals concerning the treatment of the children while in their mother's care. Didn't child protective services mention some bruises?"

Benjamin looked up, saw JC standing in the doorway, and motioned for her to come in.

"I have to go; I'll be in the office early tomorrow until about 11:00. Call Mr. Conway now, and see if he has eaten etc as we talked about and if you have to, go over there tonight. That gives him one more day before the next court hearing. Tomorrow then." He clicked off the phone, stood up went to JC.

"All settled in?" Linking his arm through hers, they went over by the glowing fireplace.

"You bet. I almost got settled in the carpet and lost in 'my room'. I have never seen such thick carpet. It felt so good on my feet." JC laughed and lifted one bare foot. She sat down on the leather loveseat patting the place next to her.

Sitting down next to her, Benjamin put his arm around her shoulders.

JC leaned back against him. "Don't you get lonely living here all alone? It's so big you ought to have a map of the condo on that table when the elevator opens." Smiling, she looked up at him.

Leaning his head down, he kissed her, "To tell you the truth, I usually spend my time in here, my bedroom and the kitchen. If I have a tough case, I've been known to sleep at the office; I have a couch, change of clothes and a shower there. I feel like I've been on my first vacation in a long time being at the mansion. I do some entertaining but not often." His voice trailed off and he leaned down and kissed her on the top of her head.

"Ahem, Benjie, I have some cheese and crackers, hot chocolate and sliced apples." Betty announced as she carried the tray and placed it on the table by the loveseat. "If you don't need anything more, I'll retire for the night."

Benjamin never moved his arm from JC' shoulder, just remained as he was. "Thank you, Betty. This very thoughtful of you. I think we are fine, sleep well." He smiled at her.

Reaching into her pocket, she removed a slip of paper and she handed it to him, "This is the names of the boutiques you might want to visit tomorrow." She nodded at both of them. "Good night."

Both JC and Benjamin at the same time said, "Good night Betty."

As Betty left the room, she mused to herself, *in all these years, I've never seen Benjie sitting with his arm around a woman unless it was for one of those photo ops, and he seems comfortable with her. Maybe she is the one for my Benjie. He has been so alone since William and Ann died. He seems so happy now. I will keep an eye on her, I don't want him hurt.*

Leaning forward, JC took a small plate and put a few crackers and cheese slices on it and apple slices. "I hate to admit it, but that snack looks good, I'm hungry already. Do you want to share with me?" She sat back and offered the plate toward him.

Nodding his head yes, Benjamin helped himself from her plate.

Silently they ate and watched the flames from the fireplace. They were comfortable with the silence. Then they settled back with the mugs of hot chocolate.

"This reminds me of the mansion in away, the fireplace, a snack, only there would be marsh mellows in my chocolate and admonitions not to spill." JC had a smile on her face. "Sometimes we'd all be on the floor resting our head on pillows and eating popcorn." She turned her face to him, "You like popcorn I hope, I eat it at least once a week."

"Yes I do, but haven't had any in a long time." Glancing at his watch, "Are you tired?"

Stifling a yawn, "How did you guess?"

"It's been a long day. I'll walk you back to your room; I wouldn't want you to get lost." Benjamin laughed reaching out for her hand.

"Just a minute," JC bent to put the dishes back on the tray, "First lead me to the kitchen."

Once in the kitchen, she rinsed the mugs out and loaded the dishes into the dishwasher, wiped off the tray and placed it on the counter. "Now, I'm ready."

Arm and arm they walked to her room stopping at the doorway.

"I'm glad you agreed to fly here with me. I hope tomorrow will turn out to be a marvelous day for us." Benjamin took her in his arms and warmly kissed her. She returned the embrace. He continued to hold her for a minute, then reluctantly released her with a sigh, "Good night my special JC."

"Night Benjamin, and thanks for the flowers." She watched him walk back down the hall, then closed the door and leaned against it. *This has been the most wonderful day.*

CHAPTER FOURTEEN

Surprised to find the dishes from last night's snack in the dishwasher and no crumbs on the coffee table in the study, Betty assumed the young lady must have cleaned up. Benjie wasn't into doing much at the house. She usually did that or the clean up staff as Benjie was always so busy with the firm.

She had just placed the oranges on the counter and was reaching for the bacon when JC entered the kitchen wearing a pretty mint green dress and her long hair held back by a clip in the back of her head.

"Good Morning. What can I do to help with breakfast?" JC walked over to her. "Um, that coffee perking smells wonderful."

This took Betty off guard. She wasn't use to offers to assist with breakfast. She liked this young lady more and more.

Opening a drawer, Betty retrieved a white apron, "Here, put this on so you don't mess up your dress and you can juice the oranges." She pointed out where the juicer, knife, and small pitcher were.

"Did you sleep well, Miss Smith?" Betty inquired.

"I'm JC, remember, and yes I did, very well." She giggled, "I have never slept in a king size bed before. Oh, and the mattress, perfect, like sleeping on a cloud," JC washed the oranges off and placed them on the cutting board.

As Benjamin walked into the kitchen dressed in his suit, ready for the office, he was surprised to see JC there too. He assumed she would be sleeping in, enjoying a day off. "Good morning, ladies. Um it smells good here.

"And a good morning to you too, Benjie, the bacon is almost done and I am poaching the eggs today if that is all right with you." Betty turned the bacon over as she was speaking.

"Fine, that's fine, Betty."

Benjamin put his arm around JC's waist, "I love fresh squeezed orange juice. Thanks for helping Betty. I thought you would be still sleeping." Then he gave her a kiss on the cheek.

JC turned her face and he kissed her on the lips. They smiled enjoying that special moment.

Betty looking out the corner of her eye smiled too. *Ah, yes, Benjie was smitten by the young lady.*

"Coffee is ready, Benjie. The creamer is on the table." Betty placed the bacon on some paper toweling.

"And here is your orange juice, oh master of the condo." JC laughed, placing his glass and hers on the table. Observing only two place settings, she asked, "Betty, aren't you joining us? I have your glass of juice, too."

Benjamin and Betty shared glances.

Betty never sat with his new guests unless it was for business.

"Yes, join us and fill us in on the latest gossip about town," Benjamin answered.

JC placed another setting on the table for Betty. "Do you drink coffee too, Betty?"

"Why, yes."

Betty joined them and they bowed their heads as Benjamin offered a blessing over the food.

"Benjie, did you get through the notes I placed on your desk?" Betty inquired.

"Yes, thank you. I did receive a lot of them at the mansion and took care of those, but that is some of the reason I'm here. Maybe I should have had you at the office to run things while I was gone." Benjamin put his hand over hers, "I don't know what I'd do without you."

Looking over at JC, he said, "Betty was my strength when mom and dad died. She really kept things from falling apart. She was my dad's personal secretary and when I took over, once I had the reins in my hand, she decided to retire. I convinced her to stay part time that she would be lost without the excitement of the office. I'm glad she did. Whenever I have a difficult case, we talk it over. I value her opinion immensely."

Betty looking at JC added, "My family are all scattered, and I loved working, so this was perfect for me. Benjie is like my own son. But if I want time off, I let him know. I have my own apartment, but when he is gone, I stay here."

"Sounds like a perfect plan to me. Everyone needs a special person in their life. Benjamin told me he had mentioned my upbringing to you. I was lucky to have my grandparents and Benjamin's grandparents as I was growing up."

Benjamin glanced at his watch, "Ladies, thank you for the lovely breakfast but I have to leave, duty calls and I told George to pick me up two minutes ago."

He looked over at JC, "The offer is still open if you want to go to the office with me. You look wonderful and I'd like you company."

JC turned to Betty, "Is this dress okay?"

Betty nodded yes, "But I think you should put on shoes."

The phone rang and Betty answered, "George, another minute and he will be right down."

Swiftly, JC went to her room, put on her heels, grabbed her purse, slipped in her gun and badge and met Benjamin at the door.

* * *

After they were buckled into the limo, JC put her hand on Benjamin's arm. "When did you get the name Benjie from Betty?"

"Actually when I was little and Mom was still doing some legal foot work for Dad, Betty would keep an eye on me as she typed up briefs and other things. One day I hurt myself and was crying and she put a bandage on my cut, cuddled me on her lap and sang to me until I calmed down and I became Benjie. Nobody else calls me that."

"How sweet, she seems like wonderful person." She squeezed his arm.

"And you, how come you are called JC instead of Janice or Janice Caroline?" Benjamin asked.

"It's weird. Either the locals called my grandpa, Sheriff Cole or CS. At my young age, I wanted to be like grandpa so I wouldn't answer unless they called me JC, because I was going to be a sheriff too like grandpa when I grew up. They humored me, figuring I'd grow out of it, but it stuck."

"So, how would you like me to introduce you today, as Miss Smith, Miss Janice Smith, or JC Smith? "His eyes filled with merriment.

"How about to those you like, I can be JC. To the others, Miss Smith will do. They will never believe the 'Smith' name and think of funny reasons as to why I'm here. Your call."

The limo pulled close to the curb. "Do you want me to wait Mr. Murphy, or park?"

Looking over at JC, "Are you going to stay with me till 11:00 or so, or would you like George to pick you up sooner and go sightseeing or something." Benjamin gave her the option.

She responded, "I'll stay here with you."

George opened the limo door, offered her a hand to exit the limo and leaning close to her whispered, "Personally I like JC, but there are a couple of snobs up there. Be Miss Smith to them." He released her hand giving her a friendly wink.

Benjamin followed JC out of the limo. "George, depending on the meetings, I will be ready between 11 and 11:30, no later. He handed him the list of boutiques Betty had given him earlier. "We will be stopping at some or all of these." Benjamin turned to JC. "Do you want to go for lunch before or after visiting a few of the shops?"

"After. We can always grab a sandwich if we get hungry. I saw many vendors out there. Let's see if we are really hungry or not when you're done here. Is that okay?"

"I'll be in the garage dusting off the limo, not circling around by 11:00, Mr. Murphy, just call me when you are ready." George gave a friendly salute and got back into the limo.

"Guess he solved it for us." Benjamin offered his arm to JC and they entered the building.

The minute they entered the suite of offices, everyone there were greeting and throwing questions at Benjamin while giving JC the once over. She didn't look like a client and she wasn't dressed in a business suit, so it didn't appear she was going to be hired.

After greeting everyone, Benjamin introduced JC. "Miss Smith is a special friend of mine." You could see the glances passing back and forth with everyone wondering how special of a friend. "I'll be here today until 11. I have plans for the rest of the day and tomorrow. The next day, I'm flying back with Miss Smith and you will email or fax me any problems that might occur as you have been doing. You are all doing a fantastic job in my absence but there are a few things I still need to take care of in Freedomville. Now, I'll see those on the Sherman case first in my office and we will go from there. Make everything brief since I did look over the cases yesterday." Benjamin took JC by the elbow and escorted her to his office.

They could hear the murmuring behind them wondering, who she was. No one noticed a ring on her finger, but he did seem very comfortable with her.

After two hours of discussions on different cases, a young woman knocked on the door and then wheeled a cart with rolls, donuts, sandwiches, some yogurt and fresh fruit on it. "Do you need any more coffee, Mr. Murphy?"

"No, this is fine, Susie. Thank you. I was starting to get a little hungry."

"It's nice to have you back, sir," and she left the room, closing the door gently behind her.

Those in the room filled plates and sat back down to eat and discuss their case. JC also fixed a plate. She was enjoying their discussions, but didn't comment on anything and understood everything she heard in that room stayed in that room, as it was confidential. This was a part of Benjamin's life she could now share in, just as Betty did.

At fifteen minutes to eleven, JC excused herself and went into the hall to find a restroom. She knew there was one in Benjamin's office, but didn't want to use that.

She closed the door and looked around. Not seeing any obvious ladies room, she walked down the hall to where they came in and greeted the receptionist there. "Hello, could you tell me where the powder room is."

The receptionist gestured in the direction to go. "To your left down the hall and it is the third door, Miss Smith."

JC nodded, and said, "Thank you." She was amazed the receptionist remembered her name.

When JC entered the bathroom, she could hear two other ladies talking. She went into an empty stall. The conversation stopped while the toilets were flushing.

The gossiping continued and she could clearly hear what they were saying as they washed their hands, "My boss said the lady that came in with Mr. Murphy stayed there the whole time, but she didn't comment on anything. He said she seemed interested in the cases, not bored at all with the legal jargon. Mr. Murphy didn't say what type of business she was in, nothing. Man, did you see her shape, she must really work out, I'd love to have her figure, and those blue eyes? The colors seem to change depending on how she looked at someone. I wonder who she is and why she is here."

"Don't worry about it. I've seen some of the ones that traipse in here inviting him to all different events in town and trust me; they never even have a hair out of place. I wonder how much they spend on plastic surgeons and salons. And their clothes, any tighter and I'd swear they were painted on."

JC waited until she heard the door close, and then left the stall. After washing her hands, she touched up her lipstick and smoothed a hand over her hair. She peered into the mirror examining her face. There was nothing glamorous about her. She had a nice complexion, didn't wear much makeup as a police officer. Wearing a hat and being in different situations, one didn't worry about a fancy hair do. Well, Benjamin liked her as she was, and that's all that counted. If he wanted a 'city' girl, she wouldn't be here.

The two women were gossiping with the receptionist when JC left the bathroom, and got a little flustered realizing JC overheard what they had said about her. As JC walked by them she casually remarked, "You're right ladies, I do work out."

She met a smiling Benjamin coming down the hall with his employees trailing behind him. "Ready to go Beautiful? George is waiting out front for us," he offered her his arm and they left the office leaving a lot of speculation about how important Miss Smith was to Mr. Murphy, the city's most eligible bachelor.

* * *

"Benjamin, we have been to every store, I mean boutique on the list Betty prepared and you have purchased at least one outfit from each one for me. I have more than enough clothes and these are so beautiful, when am I to wear them all? My feet are killing me from trying on all those high heels. Let's go." JC's pleaded with him.

"My dear, you will occasions to wear them all when you are with me, or presiding at functions in the mansion. I have one more place I want to take you, it is an exclusive store and her designs are recognized by everyone. They have lovely gowns for the concerts I want us to go to. Matter of fact, I have tickets for tomorrow night. One more shop then we will call it a day. I promise." He picked up her hand and kissed it.

The action didn't go unnoticed by the sales ladies. They didn't care, his credit card was good and he tipped them well, very well. Working on commission, those large tips really were appreciated.

George carried out the latest purchases and stacked them in the back with the others.

They quickly arrived at the designated place, The House of Cheree, where only wealthy people could afford to shop and most of them were snobs that had never worked a day in their life.

If JC was over whelmed with the prices on the other clothes, she felt these were absolutely sinful. She leaned over and whispered to Benjamin, "One, I shouldn't be letting you buy these clothes for me and two, they are way too expensive."

"One, I can afford it, I'm a lawyer not a cop, and two, it makes me happy and you look so beautiful wearing them. Let me do this for you." Benjamin's face got very serious, "JC, I think we both know we are heading for something special, and when we are here in New York, no one will hold a candle to you when we go to occasions requiring formal dress. And when we are in Freedomville, we wear what is appropriate for there. Okay?"

"Okay." She knew he was right. No way could she afford these dresses and she knew they were past the 'I like you' phase.

The sales clerk walked slowly toward them with an exaggerated sway as though she were regal and stopped in front of JC. "Miss, we have the elegant ensemble ready Mr. Murphy has chosen for you to try on. I'm sure you will look simply marvelous in it." She gestured for JC to follow her.

JC turned around with a look of 'this is the last one I'm trying on'.

Benjamin just smiled.

About five minutes later, JC appeared wearing a lovely sapphire blue strapless gown with very simple lines that flowed with her when she walked. The silver high heel sandals and diamond accessories completed the look of elegance. Over her arm, she carried a very light lacy shawl, if needed. Someone had put her hair up with a few light strands loose by her ears.

Benjamin stood up as she got closer. The look on his face told her this was the dress.

"Beautiful, simply beautiful, JC. You will be my princess at dinner tonight."

JC blushed, and curtsied. "Thank you, Prince Charming."

Benjamin looked over at the clerk who was standing back, pleased with herself for picking out the most expensive outfit in the place. Mentally she was adding up what the complete ensemble Mr. Murphy had selected cost, and her commission.

"Wrap it up, including the accessories," Benjamin instructed the very happy clerk, as she walked quickly, not regally this time, back to help JC get undressed.

As George picked up the boxes to take out to the limo, he leaned in close to Benjamin, "I hope you're done shopping Mr. Murphy, 'cause I'm running out of room in the limo. Any more boxes and they are riding shotgun up front with me."

"That we are, George. That we are."

On the ride back to the condominium Benjamin took JC's hand, "If you aren't too exhausted from shopping, I would like for us to go out for a late dinner and you wear one of your new dresses. I think right now, a time to relax would be good for both of us... unless you want to work out in my home gym."

"I love that idea, working out I mean, do you know how tiring it is trying on all those clothes and clerks fawning all over you? Exercising to work up a sweat is also relaxing, then a shower and dress up time. Do you want to join me, for the workout I mean, not the shower?" JC smiled at him. "Man, I don't know how women can spend so much time shopping, trying on clothes and walking in high heels and say they enjoy it. That is more tiring than working my shift. But, you have to pick out which dress I'm to wear. I don't know the place you're taking me and I don't want to be over dressed."

"Yes to the work out, but let Betty help you pick out the dress for dinner."

JC cocked her head to one side, "I have another question; George drives the limo, George needs to go home, are you going to drive the limo?"

Benjamin burst out laughing. "No, my dear, we will use the limo service that the condo provides."

The limo came to a stop and George turned around in his seat, "Well you two are safely back to the castle. I'll bring your packages up Miss Smith." He turned back, got out and opened their door. "I'll probably get a hernia from lifting all these boxes though."

They all burst out laughing.

George brought all the boxes up to the sixth floor on a rolling cart and Benjamin handed him the tickets for the concert and slipped some extra cash to George.

"Mr. Murphy, no need for that. You pay me well enough." George handed back the folded up bills to Benjamin.

"Take your wife to dinner and then the theater. Stop on your way home and get her some flowers. You work odd hours for me, and your wife is very understanding and George, I appreciate that. Have a good night. I'll call you tomorrow and let you know what time I will need you."

"Thank you, sir." George tipped his hat at Benjamin and left.

* * *

Betty stopped at the entrance of the den, "You wanted to see me, Benjie?"

"Yes, come in and close the door, please. Where is JC?"

"She's soaking in the whirlpool. She can't get over all the new clothes you got her. She is like a little girl at Christmas time. I have them all hung up." Betty took a seat by the desk.

Benjamin slid a legal envelope over to her. "I want you to read this."

Betty picked it up, opened it and read through it. She looked up at him, "Are you sure you want to do this Benjie? It's part of your heritage. It has been such a short time since you became aware of your grandfather and all and, do you really know her that well? I've seen how the young ladies and their mothers are constantly trying to interest you in them. Does JC know how much you are worth?"

Getting out of his chair Benjamin walked around his desk and knelt down by her. "I value your opinion very much. You are family to me. I didn't know my grandfather, but JC did. She loves the mansion. To me, it doesn't have that feeling. I told you about grandfather's wishes we found in the desk, and to dangle it in front of her isn't right. I love her, Betty. I know it has all happened quickly. I have never had any loving feeling for anyone like I do for her. I don't like to be apart from her. I want to marry her, but I don't want her to feel any strings are attached to my proposal plus I don't need the money from any of the property. And the answer to your question, no, she doesn't know how much I am worth, and you know, she wouldn't care if I didn't have a dime."

Tapping her manicured finger against the deed, "Money isn't everything is it, Benjie? I'm glad you realize that. I have seen how you look at JC. It's the first time you have ever been this serious about someone. Well, Benjie, you are a successful attorney, what would you tell a client in a situation like this?"

Standing up, Benjamin smiled, "I'd tell him to have a detective investigate her to make sure she wasn't a gold digger. Trust me; JC is a hard working police officer, a good person. She is going to be coming into some money that was put into a trust soon by her grandfather after her parents died. I think she has forgotten about it. She has integrity, she is a good Christian, and people in that small town love her."

"If, I'm just wondering, if you two decided to break up, will you regret losing some of your history?" Betty questioned concern showing in her eyes.

He shook his head. "Like I said, the mansion was a second home to her; she knows every crook and cranny of it. She is comfortable there, and has so many memories." Benjamin smiled. "What's money, Betty?" He bent down and gave her a hug. "Love you, thanks."

CHAPTER FIFTEEN

The news reporter put down his drink, clicked his pen and flipped over a new page as he watched the reaction of the women as Benjamin Murphy from the prestigious Murphy Law Firm entered the room with a raving beauty on his arm. She was wearing a striking blue gown from The House of Cheree, the most expensive boutique in town, and she wore it well.

Heads were turning and people whispered speculating who the stranger was with the rich Mr. Murphy. Envy was evident in the eyes of eligible women who were constantly seeking his attention. So far, Mr. Murphy had escaped the clutches of the many mommas' trying to catch a rich husband for their daughters.

He watched intently as the couple was ushered to a table that was more secluded. He chuckled, at the adoration on Mr. Murphy's face as he looked at the mystery woman. If it was genuine, wedding bells wouldn't be too long in the future.

Man, she was a looker. The bare arms and good posture showed she worked out. Nothing about her suggested a plastic surgeon had been anywhere near her and she didn't have her face plastered with enough make up to camouflage any flaws.

Even with the slow walk to the table, she showed poised and strength. Somehow, he didn't sense she was looking for a meal ticket.

I'd give a week's wages to have a woman give me that look she just gave him. I need to have a chat with that Benjamin Murphy; he must be taking something to ooze out that much masculine charm. He looked down at his abundant abdomen and sighed. Finishing his drink, he motioned to the waiter for another. His tomorrow's gossip column would be great.

* * *

After the waiter took their order, JC spoke softly, "I feel like I'm on display. Is everyone in this town that rude to gawk at me?"

Benjamin took her hand in his and kissed it. "Ignore them, Beautiful; it's like this all the time when there is an eligible bachelor around. Just wait, anyone who is a parent with a daughter of marrying age will soon be stopping by to check out the competition say hello and get a closer look at you and an introduction."

"You're kidding, right? They would interrupt our meal?"

"Don't look now JC, but our first *interruption* is about to make a stop." He kept his hand over JC's.

"Good evening, Benjamin. We haven't seen you around town lately." She spoke to Benjamin but was giving JC the once over.

Benjamin stood up, "I've been out of town on business, which happens in my line of work you know." He looked down at JC. "My dear, this is Mrs. Carson and her daughter, Darlene. Ladies, my dear friend, Miss Janice Smith." He glanced over by their table, "Oh, I see your meal is being served. It was nice of you to stop by, have a nice evening." He sat down once more taking JC's hand in his.

Use to being the center of attention and wanting to put Benjamin's date in her place as not one of their circle, Darlene leaned over, resting her hands on the table exposing a view of her voluptuous breasts that were spilling over from her low cut gown. She knew that would get his attention, big boobs always got a man's attention. "Bye Benjamin," Completely ignoring JC but kept eye contact with Benjamin, she spoke in a low intimate tone, "I'll call you later, mommy is having a dinner party next week. All our friends will be there, it should be lots of fun. I hope you can come." She stood up slowly and tossed her long platinum colored hair over her shoulder giving him a sexy look.

Embarrassed at her daughter's rude behavior, Mrs. Carson took a firm hold on her daughter's arm, "Come Darlene, our dinner is waiting." They had to leave or look ridiculous standing there considering Benjamin had sat down.

As the two women left their table, JC smiled at him, "They are smarting because you didn't give them my autobiography. They will probably get indigestion now from their dinner."

They both chuckled and sent a glance toward the Carson table.

Their dinner arrived, their water glasses refilled, and they were watched, but everyone else left them alone. If Mrs. Carson got nowhere in finding out the low down on his companion, they best wait awhile. It wasn't healthy to irritate a wealthy, single bachelor. Who know, this unknown female might just be a fling.

After JC and Benjamin finished their meal, they went to the dance floor. All eyes were riveted on them, but the two lovebirds ignored them as they moved gracefully with the romantic music.

A tap on Benjamin's shoulder indicated someone wanted to dance with JC. She looked at Benjamin with a question in her eyes. Benjamin nodded an okay, and introduced Mike Dawson, a reporter and backed away to the edge of the dance floor.

The overweight reporter took her hand in his sweaty one and for a fat man was light on his feet. "So, what's your name?"

"Miss Smith."

"Where are you from, I haven't seen you around here before." *He was getting out of breath even with the slow dance. He really needed to diet.*

"I'm from out of town." JC replied, grateful that the music stopped. She quickly dropped her hand from his, adjusted the thin strap of the small silver purse over her shoulder and walked toward Benjamin. They wove their way back to their table, ignoring the music for another slow dance.

"Okay, JC?"

"Yeah, it was just a twenty question dance but he only got two in." She laughed, "He found out my name is Miss Smith and I am from out of town. Guess he won't get a job as a detective."

"Ah, but my dear, Mike works for one of the major newspapers. Don't underestimate the power of a reporter. Check out the papers tomorrow and in his column he will no doubt have the type of perfume you are wearing, what size dress you had on, where it came from, that you are a lovely dancer and I am one lucky guy." Benjamin smiled. "Welcome to New York where nothing is secret or sacred. If they don't know the truth, they make up something…and if it is juicy, the better. Now, let's give them something to really talk about." He leaned over and kissed her lightly on the lips.

You could hear the intake of breaths in the room.

Smiling, JC looked up at him, "I think these people have way too much money and time on their hands and need to get a life. I'm tired of being the object of their conversation. Can we go now?"

He nodded and gestured to the waiter. He gave him the credit card and signed for the bill.

* * *

The heavy reporter watched as they left the room. *Um, I wonder why she danced with her small handbag and didn't leave it at the table. It seemed rather heavy for just holding the usual lipstick and cell phone. Maybe she is from the sticks and things are done differently there, but she has class. He chuckled to himself as he recalled how the spoiled Miss Darlene Carson's seductive action didn't get the response she was expecting. It was going to be an interesting season if Miss Smith, assuming that was her name, remained in New York.*

He quickly paid his bill leaving a healthy tip since waiters and waitresses were a good source of information, and discreetly followed the handsome couple. He might over hear something as they waited for their ride. He knew Mr. Murphy had his own driver and limousine.

* * *

As the two stepped outside and waited for the limo to come, JC was commenting on how good it felt to have the cool air to breathe and be away from all those prying eyes when a man came running across the busy street, dodging vehicles while waving a hand gun in the air shouting, "You rich bastard, why didn't you get my kid off? He's locked up for life, might as well say he is dead. Well, I'm not going to pay you, you're going to pay, you're gonna be dead too!"

Instinctively removing her gun from the dressy silver purse, JC assumed a stance and shouted, "Police! Drop your gun! Now! Drop your gun or I'll shoot!"

Instead, the angry man squeezed the trigger and Benjamin fell to the ground with a thud. JC took careful aim and shot the raving man in the arm that was holding the gun before he could squeeze the trigger again. Dropping the gun he grabbed his arm and screamed out obscenities at her. A cabbie kicked the gun away and subdued the man. Soon sirens were heard wailing in the distance.

Kneeling down by Benjamin, JC asked, "Where does it hurt?" She unbuttoned his suit jacket; the right side of his white shirt was now red. Pulling his shirt out of his suit pants she saw a side wound. Taking his handkerchief, she pressed it against the bleeding hole.

"I think you will be okay, it smarts though doesn't it?" She turned her head listening, "From the sounds of it, help is arriving." Leaning over she kissed him.

"Not the evening I had planned, JC."

"Hush. Just lie still."

"What's going on here?" A gruff voice demanded.

JC stood up. "Office Smith from Freedomville. That man over there," she pointed at the swearing man, "was waving his gun and threatening, Benjamin Murphy, the injured man. I identified myself as Officer Smith ordering him to put down his gun instead he shot Mr. Murphy. I shot the perpetrator in the arm not knowing if he would keep shooting or not."

"Give me your gun; I don't care where you're from, you're coming down to the station with me." The officer held out his hand for it.

JC gave him the gun. Never blinking an eye, "I have my badge and ID card here too. I'll come to the station after I go to the hospital with Benjamin. Better yet, come with us and he can give his statement and I'll make out my report. But I am going to the hospital first with him." *This might be the big city of New York, but unless they cuffed her, she was going with her Benjamin.*

Two men in white scrubs quickly brought a gurney over, assisted Benjamin to his feet, and onto the gurney. JC walked with them, turning to see the other injured man getting into a different ambulance. That was good.

Other police officers were asking questions of the people milling around.

Officer Johnson kept step with her. They were riding in the ambulance with Benjamin and he wasn't letting her out of his sight. Mr. Murphy was well known in the city, but who this Officer Smith was, he'd have to check out. Besides, they would need to test her for alcohol and drugs with a blood and urine test and her clothes taken for evidence. This was New York City, not MAYBERRY, USA.

* * *

As the ambulances with lights flashing, pulled away, the heavyset reporter quickly shut his notebook and waved for a taxi, he had a fantastic article to write and it might make front page... not the society section this time, but first he had to follow that ambulance, for the rest of the story.

CHAPTER SIXTEEN

The area around the reception desk was crowded with clamoring reporters trying to get any information they could about Mr. Murphy, the prominent attorney, disregarding the ill patients waiting to be registered. Finally, after ignoring the receptionists request that leave the area, the hospital security guards told them to move on or they would all be arrested. None of the security noticed the heavyset man that stayed quietly over by the wall not far from the conversing police officers.

Back in the inner workings of the ER, JC and Officer Johnson sat on cold straight chairs along the wall waiting for the doctors to finish taking care of Benjamin.

A nurse came out with a small plastic bag holding Benjamin's personal things and handed them to JC. The bag with the bloody clothes she gave to Officer Johnson. "I don't know if the dry cleaners will be able to get all the blood out when you are done with it." She looked over at JC, "It looks like your dress will be hard to clean too. We would appreciate it if you bring those scrubs you were loaned back to us tomorrow."

JC looked down at the bag holding her beautiful expensive gown with the front full of blood from kneeling down next to

Benjamin when she kissed him. Dresses could be replaced; she was more concerned about Benjamin.

Officer Johnson moved away from her, talking discreetly on the phone. Then without a word to her, he went through the swinging doors. A few minutes later, he returned with another officer and a clipboard.

"Officer Smith, please fill out this report. I need to see your Police ID now."

JC removed a holder from her small purse that held her driver's license, Police ID, one credit card and a ten-dollar bill. He wrote down the needed numbers.

The second officer disappeared and JC filled out the forms necessary any time a police officer had to shoot anyone with their weapon on duty or not.

Johnson's phone rang. "A ha, okay, right."

He sat back down by JC. Taking the completed forms she had filled out, "We have talked with your captain and he knows you are now officially on leave until our investigation is done. You may not leave the city. You realize that your position as a police officer isn't recognized in our city. You will need an attorney. I will be forwarding this case to the District Attorney who will determine if this was a justified shooting or not. If they determine it isn't a justifiable shooting, you will be charged. Do you understand?"

"Yes. I know that is standard procedure."

Officer Johnson continued, "What is the address and phone number of where you are currently staying?"

"Just a minute." JC replied opening the bag that holding Benjamin's personal items, she removed his black billfold, opened it showing his driver's license to Officer Johnson. "It's a condo, we just flew in yesterday and I don't know the name of the building or the address. Matter of fact, I don't know the phone number and I left my cell phone back there. You can get that from Benjamin. Betty should be there if you call."

He handed back the billfold. As she went to return it, she noticed the envelope in the bag had her name on it. She picked it up, with a puzzled look on her face she remarked to Officer Johnson. "This must have been inside of his suit jacket. He never said anything to me about it."

The envelope was official light beige colored with a smear of blood on it. It had Attorney Jensen's return address on it, but it was addressed to her. *Why would Benjamin have a letter addressed to her? Um there was no stamp or postmark.* She opened it up removing three sheets of paper. One was a letter from Mr. Jensen; the other two were deeds, one for the mansion and the other for the attached farm acreage in her name. Tears filled her eyes and she started to cry silently, her shoulders shaking,

Officer Johnson pulled out some tissues from a box on a table and handed them to her. "Are you okay? What's the bad news?"

JC shook her head, "No bad news, a very unselfish gift of love." She wiped her eyes and blew her nose. "Excuse me a minute, I want to read this."

She read the letter from Mr. Jensen.

Dear Janice Caroline Smith,

Mr. Benjamin Murphy came into my office the morning after reading the letter his deceased grandfather, Mr. Willard Murphy had concealed in the desk. The request had been written after the will was drafted and signed and wasn't a legal document. However, it is Benjamin's desire that his grandfather's wishes be honored even though they weren't stated in the will nor were there any signatures of witnesses to the letter.

Not wanting you to live in limbo always wondering if you would or wouldn't inherit the mansion and attached farm, Benjamin Murphy has deeded this over to you with no strings attached. He feels your love and memories of the mansion are very important to you. The attached farm should produce enough income to take care of any expenses to maintain the mansion that wouldn't be possible on your current wages as a police officer.

Mr. Benjamin Murphy signed the necessary papers and I had it recorded at the courthouse. It is yours.

As a friend of the family, I will share the parting words Benjamin said the day he requested this be done. "I have feelings for JC I've never felt for anyone. I am in love with her. I know she will never do anything to damage what she loves. Grandfather should have given it to her in the first place." I don't feel this was privileged information since everyone can see how he feels about you.
Yours truly,

Arthur Jensen
Attorney at Law

JC sat very still absorbing what she had just read. It didn't seem real. She looked at the deeds again. Her name, all hers, no leans, no ands, ifs, or buts, hers.

"Hey, you okay?" Officer Johnson touched her arm. "You realize that is a piece of evidence." He paused, looking at her. "What is it?"

"A gift, the deed to the home I spent my life in and the farm around it." She handed it for him to read.

When he finished, he gave it back. "Sounds like a nice present."

Nodding her head, she slowly folded the papers, put them back into the envelope and replaced it back inside the clear plastic bag.

Officer Johnson let her. He knew if he took them, it could be months before she got them back and in his estimation, she only did what she was trained for: stop an angry man from injuring or killing anyone. If, the investigation showed she purposely shot the man... he'd take the heat for not taking the envelope now.

The nurse came out from Benjamin's room, "You may talk with the patient now."

They both stood up and followed her. JC was surprised to see Benjamin conscious.

"Hi Beautiful, sorry our evening ended this way, and your dress got ruined, but you look really cool in those scrubs." Benjamin smile faded when he noticed she had been crying.

Pushing forward, "I'm Officer Johnson." The police officer pointed at his own badge, "Sorry you were shot. Mr. Murphy. Were you given any medication that made you lose consciousness?"

Benjamin smiled, "No, just a local shot to numb the pain as they probed a bit. The bullet went through not damaging any internal organs or bones. They have x-rayed me, cleaned out the wound, given me numerous shots for infection and I am just receiving some fluids to replace the lost blood. When that is done, I can go home. Now, start with your questions officer."

Office Johnson was impressed with Benjamin. The fact that he was a lawyer showed he was ready for business and cool under pressure. Looking down at his notes, the officer commented, "According to witnesses, you evidently know the perpetrator since he blamed you for his son going to jail. When was the last time you saw him? Has he threatened you before?"

"No, he has never threatened me. My firm does a few cases for indigent people. This was one of them. I prefer the newer lawyers work with poverty cases since they have school loans to pay themselves and understand the money crunch more and work hard for the client. I always sit in with them, monitoring, but they are in charge.

Mr. Lentz came to us because his son Arty was in trouble. He got in with the wrong people, was doing drugs and while under the influence, Arty and three other men beat a man to death, stole his wallet, credit cards and car. This wasn't his first run in with the law, but none had been as serious as this one. The jury said guilty. For some reason, Mr. Lentz thought we could wave a magic wand and get his son off scot-free. I can't prove it, but I wonder if some of the illegal money didn't filter down to dad is why he took such irrational action tonight? I really never noticed any closeness to each other."

Looking down at his note pad, Officer Johnson spoke, "My note says Mr. Lentz said he wasn't going to pay you, yet you say you do this free gratis. Did you give him a bill?"

"No, he didn't receive any bill. Some clients that are on the borderline of low income, we may give them a bill for twenty-five dollars. That way they don't feel like they are a parasite. They are the hard workers at low pay, and really can't afford an attorney but don't qualify for a court appointed one."

The nurse knocked on the open door, "There is a chauffeur by the name of George asking if you are here? Are you?" She smiled. Hospital confidentiality rules had to be followed.

"Of course, have him come in." Benjamin replied. Looking at JC he asked, "Did you call him?"

Laughing softly, "Benjamin, I don't know the phone number for George or as a matter of fact, the condo."

Benjamin gave Officer Johnson his home and work number which the officer slowly wrote down in his small notebook, repeating them back to Benjamin insuring accuracy.

Slipping the pad and pen into his shirt pocket, "I'll be in touch Mr. Murphy if I have any more questions," turning to face JC, "And Miss Smith, remember, don't leave town."

As Officer Johnson left the room, George entered, hat in hand, concern covering his face. "My wife and I were on our way to the theater and got stopped by the police blocking the road at the restaurant. The driver of the condo limo text me about the shooting and I told him he could leave, that I'd be making sure you got home okay if they didn't keep you. I tried to get to you Mr. Murphy, but with all the police cars and all..." his voice trailed away.

"Understandable, George, not to worry, you're here now in time to take us back home. By the way, how did you know which hospital I would be at?" Benjamin looked up at the nurse who was discontinuing his IV.

"Process of elimination, the first ambulance with you and Miss Smith in it, headed this direction, the other one went the other way." George looked around and leaning toward them said in a quiet voice, "They sure are hardnosed about giving any information out front even when I told them who I was. And for the record, I saw that heavyset reporter out front too, you know the one who writes what my wife calls, the gossip column."

"Guess that means I'll be the topic in tomorrow's paper. He was at the restaurant too and even got a few minutes of a dance with JC."

A receptionist interrupted them with a clipboard holding the sign out papers and an appointment set up for Benjamin to see his regular physician in three days unless he had any signs of infection. She also had a clean shirt and hospital scrub bottoms he could wear home.

"JC, if you would kindly step out, George will help me get dressed. I for one want to go home."

JC nodded and stepped out to the hall. *She needed to get phone numbers of Benjamin's condo, the firm, Betty, and George and when they got back to the condo, she needed to call a few people at home and let them know what happened before they heard it on the news. The news! No telling what that obese reporter would write. She sighed, what a night. At least Benjamin would be okay, and that was the main thing. Her Benjamin.*

* * *

Mike Dawson, the reporter hailed a cab. Once again staying quietly in the background, he got the information he needed when those dumb flat-footed police officers talked to loud on the phone and to each other.

He chuckled to himself; so the quiet little lady was a cop herself, from some small berg of a town. He knew her purse was too heavy when they had that short dance, now he knew why, the hottie was packin', and she was a cop. For some reason that didn't come as a surprise to him, maybe it was the way she carried herself, with confidence. Man she sure is a looker, more like a model than a crime fighter. I wonder where Murphy found her and were there any more that gorgeous at home like her? That would be enough for him to finally go on a diet.

The cab pulled up at the newspaper building. For a fat man he quickly got out of the back seat, tossed the cabbie some bills and swiping his ID badge, let himself into the newspaper building. He had a great story to write.

CHAPTER SEVENTEEN

Once Betty got over the shock of seeing Benjie in hospital clothes assisted by George on one side and JC in blue scrubs on the other side of him, she took charge.

Giving JC an irritated look, "You go take a shower and get out of those blue things while George and I get Benjie into his pajamas and to bed." *If JC had never come to New York, none of this would have happened!* With that, she took the arm JC had been holding and the three of them slowly walked down the hall to Benjie's room.

JC was surprised at being dismissed so rudely as she watched the three make their way down to Benjamin's room. She couldn't understand Betty had treating her that way. Everything was fine when they left for dinner.

With a deep sigh, she entered her room walking straight to the bedroom; dropped her purse on the bed, and entered the bathroom. The wall of mirrors let her see what a mess she was with her hair hanging in strands with flecks of blood in it. Her pale face with smudged make up looked back at her. She remembered standing there hours ago surprised at how the beautiful dress made her feel like a princess, and now, she sighed.

Taking off the floppy throngs and loaned scrubs, she folded them up and placed them on the floor.

She stood under the warm shower trying to relax when she realized this was the first time she had ever been in a situation requiring her to shoot anyone. The police department always practice for difficult events, but she had never been in a situation where using her gun had been necessary. The reality that she could have killed him upset her. Her tears mingled with the spray from the shower. When the gun went off and she heard Benjamin fall, she did what she had been trained to do not knowing if the gunman would keep shooting and others in the crowd or herself would be injured or killed.

Stepping out of the shower, she wrapped a towel around her head and slipped into one of the soft cotton robes and sat down on a chair still confused by Betty's unexpected angry attitude toward her, like this assault on Benjamin was all her fault. Drying off, she quickly dressed. She had calls to make and then she needed to check on Benjamin, no matter what Betty would say.

***

George assisted Benjamin into his pajamas and dressing gown then over Betty's objections, walked with him to the study and lit the fireplace as Benjamin had requested.

"George, it's time you go home to your wife. She must be wondering what is going on. I thank you immensely for you concern and help." Benjamin smiled at him. "I'm all right, really. I've got JC and Betty here and a couple of pain pills if I need them."

"Call me if you need anything, Mr. Murphy, day or night. I'm sorry this had to happen, but I'm sure glad Miss JC was there or you might not be with us anymore." George shook his head, "Well, have a good night, sir."

"Night, George."

The elevator door closed as JC opened her door. She needed to talk with Benjamin. She found him in the study resting comfortably in the recliner, his head leaning back and his eyes closed. She observed him for a minute, he didn't seem to be in pain and his color was good.

Walking over to him, "You look pretty comfy. Can I get you anything, some water or tea?" She gave him a kiss on the top of his head.

From the doorway, Betty answered in a cold formal voice for Benjamin, "I have his tea here. You can go to your room; I'm taking care of Benjie." She placed the tray on the coffee table turned to face JC with hands on her hips and she wasn't smiling.

Benjamin groaned inwardly, he knew he had a problem on his hands.

JC didn't want a confrontation but she couldn't understand why this sudden hostility towards her from Betty and wanted an answer.

"Betty, I know you are upset about Benjamin being injured, but for the life of me, I don't understand why you are angry with me. I didn't shoot him." JC reached out for her, "We both can be here for Benjamin."

Betty shrugged off JC's hand. "If you weren't here, none of this would have happened. Why are you here, trying to get a rich husband? Steal his inheritance?"

"Betty! Enough!" Benjamin slowly rose from the recliner. He put one arm around her and reached his other for JC. "I love you both. This behavior isn't necessary or acceptable. If JC hadn't been here tonight, I would in all probability be dead, shot to death by an upset man, and who knows how many others hurt or killed. She saved my life. You should be grateful. Now, Betty, would you please bring the envelope to me that is in the small plastic bag the hospital put my personal things into." He removed his arm away from her but patted her shoulder.

Benjamin watched as she left the room in a stiff angry mood, then turned and put both arms around JC hugging her close.

With her face against his chest, in a muffled voice she sobbed, "I didn't mean to cause any problems, I love you Benjamin, but I think I should leave and get a hotel room. You will heal better in a harmonious atmosphere. I can't stay here with all this feeling of discord; Betty loves you too and will take care of you. For some reason, she resents or feels threatened by me and I don't know why."

Betty stood quietly unobserved at the door listening and watching the couple.

"JC, I don't want you to leave, I want this to be our second home," putting her an arm's length away, he looked intently at her. "Don't you understand how much you mean to me? I've loved you from the first time I saw you. I can't explain it, but I would be loss without you. I know now how dad felt about my mom. Please don't leave me." He pulled her close kissing her with emotion.

Ashamed, tears ran down Betty's face as she realized what a jealous fool she had been.

Benjamin looked up and saw Betty tightly hugging the plastic bag against her chest, sadness and tears on her face. He raised his arm for her to come and she did.

"I'm sorry, Benjie and JC."

"I think this has been a very emotional evening for all of us." JC hugged Betty.

"Ladies, I need to sit down and we need to work together." He reached for the plastic bag and gently sat down. Both of the women took a chair on each side of him.

"Betty, you have been like a mother to me since mom and dad died; my confidant, my advisor. I love you." He turned to JC, "And you my lady, have stolen my heart. I want us to be a family, a family that trusts each other and cares for each other." He smiled at them, "And we will."

Retrieving the manila envelope, from the plastic bag, Benjamin handed it to JC.

Nervously she stood up turning to face him, tapping the envelope against her other hand, "I have to be honest, Benjamin, when the nurse brought your things out, the police officer needed your address and when I took out your wallet to get the information, I saw the envelope and since my name was on it, I opened it. I appreciate this unselfish gesture. Yes, I love the mansion, I have many wonderful memories, but this is your inheritance, a part of your history, your break from this fast-paced city. I can't accept it." She handed it back to him.

He refused to take it; instead, he patted a place next to him. "Please sit down. This evening was to be a nice dinner, dancing, a ride through the city and a glass of wine here, in this room where," he reached into the pocket of his robe and brought out a velvet box and opened it. "Where I was going to get down on one knee and asked you to marry me, to make my life complete." Removing the ring from the silk fabric, he poised it by her hand, "Will you Janice Caroline Smith be my wife? I love you dearly."

JC looked at the huge sparkling diamond, and then raised her eyes to look at his. She saw love in them; she felt love for him, but everything was moving so fast. "Are you sure Benjamin? Do we really know each other well enough, who we really are?"

As Benjamin slid the ring on her finger, "That's what engagements are for, time to see if there are any ghosts or old boyfriends or girlfriends in the closet. How we handle stress, finances, discuss the future, is it just a physical attraction or the real thing. No game playing. That's another reason why I gave you the mansion and farm; I didn't want any carrots dangled in front of you. No matter what happens, the mansion is yours. I love you, marry me."

In a few short seconds, memories of being with Benjamin flashed through her mind. The bottom line, yes, she did love him. Leaning forward with tears in her eyes, she responded with a husky, "Yes," and kissed him, sealing her response.

Being a spectator of the proposal, her resentment toward JC gone, Betty was touched and clapping her hands, rose up and embraced the couple, "Congratulations."

CHAPTER EIGHTEEN

Always an early riser, Betty pushed the start button on the coffee maker and went to retrieve the morning newspaper. Opening it to the front page, she gasped, "Oh my goodness." She sat down on the bench by the elevator. Tears caused the print to blur.

In large capital letters above a picture of Benjamin laying on the ground, and JC kneeling by him, both covered in blood, she felt remorse that she had been so mean to JC last night.

PROMINENT ATTORNEY SAVED BY POLICEWOMAN SWEETHEART

By Mike Dawson

Last night, as Benjamin Murphy, President of Murphy Law Firm was leaving a popular restaurant; an angry man raced across the busy street brandishing a weapon and shouting at him. Ignoring the command to drop his gun, Mr. Lentz shot Mr. Murphy in his right side. No doubt Mr. Murphy's life was saved by his beautiful date who stopped the armed man from pulling the trigger again by shooting him in the arm. This mystery woman who has been escorted about town by Mr. Murphy has been identified as a police officer, JC Smith from the small town of Freedomville. After treatment at the Emergency Center, Mr. Murphy was released.

Mr. Lentz is very lucky the bullet struck Mr. Murphy where it did or he could have been charged with murder. Witnesses said that the perpetrator was angry that the Murphy Law Firm wasn't able to keep his son from going to prison on a murder charge.

The beautiful blue gown that Officer Smith wore from The House Cheree's was covered with blood when she went to assist Mr. Murphy who was lying on the ground.

Before this tragic event, yours truly was fortunate to have a dance with the lady of the hour at the Rainbow Room in the Rock Center.

We wish Mr. Murphy a speedy recovery.

"Oh my gosh! Benjie, Benjie!" Betty raced down the hall to his bedroom.

Hearing the excited voice of Betty, JC quickly put on a robe and went to see what was going on, fearful that something had happened to Benjamin during the night.

She reached the open door to his room to see both of their heads together as they read the paper. They looked up as she entered.

"Well, we made the news. I told you your dancing reporter would have you in the paper today but I didn't expect the front page. I wonder how he got all the names. Bet he overheard the policemen." Benjamin smiled at her. "Good morning, sweetheart. Sit with me." As she sat down, he leaned over and they shared a kiss.

The phone rang and for the next hour, Betty was kept busy answering and taking messages from friends and those from the firm checking on Ben's condition. Then one call came and it was for JC, a Mr. Hermanson. Betty held her hand over the mouthpiece, "Do you want to take this call, JC?"

Nodding affirmative, she wasn't surprised at his call. After JC had called her captain last night and explained her side of what happened, where she was staying and the house phone number. She was instructed to keep him informed on what was happening. She also called Harold so he wouldn't worry and told him where a key was hidden so he could take some things out of the refrigerator that would spoil, have the post office hold her mail and also let Mr. Jensen know what was going on.

She took the phone from Betty hoping that everything was okay with John.

"Hello Harold, is everything okay with John?"

"Yes, Dad is okay, it's Tim." There was a long pause, "I don't know how to say this, I'm so embarrassed, but Tim left the Alcohol Assessment unit, slipped out somehow, and, well, darn it JC, he broke into your house and really threw things around. The place is a mess. I'll pay for all the damages." There was a suppressed sob, "He went too far this time JC, he's going to be locked up for a long time. The Captain said you can't come back here now but he is going to fax you papers to sign. I'm so sorry, so sorry."

JC stood there stunned and looked over at Benjamin and Betty. "Harold, just a minute." She held the receiver against her chest and quickly related Harold's message.

Benjamin calmly advised her, "Tell him to take pictures, have your insurance man come over and assess it, then leave everything until we get there."

"Harold, Benjamin said to take pictures, contact my insurance man Don, his number is by my phone and have him come over and look it over, leave the mess until we get back. I think the investigation on my shooting should be taken care of quickly so hopefully it shouldn't be too long. There were enough witnesses to it all. I will have to come back as a witness for the trial concerning Mr. Lentz though."

Her voice registered concern as she asked, "Harold, you didn't tell John did you, I don't want him stressed out."

"JC, you know dad, someone would blab it out, so I thought it was best I told him especially since he had been asking when you two were coming back home. He took it okay after threatening to teach Tim some lessons. Thanks for asking. Keep in touch my dear and I'll call you later." He hung up.

JC put the phone down. "Is there anything else that could possibly go wrong? You get shot, the most beautiful dress I've ever worn in my life is ruined, we are on the front page of the newspaper and now my home is trashed."

"You have me." Benjamin put out his arms and she went to him.

"Did you forget JC, you also have the mansion, your new home." Betty added. "Besides, depending on how much damage was done to the house, you will either have to have it razed or if you repair it, you can rent it out or sell it. The main thing is both of you are alive, engaged with many plans to make. Now, I don't know about you two, but I am in dire need of a cup of coffee, strong coffee."

"Ditto," JC and Benjamin said in together. They all laughed, relieving the tension and each one reached for a coffee mug.

CHAPTER NINETEEN

For some reason, JC wasn't nervous as she watched the three officials confer with the verdict of her action in the shooting. Even though she wasn't on duty, or in the New York Police System, she had conducted herself as an officer of the law when confronted with a dangerous situation.

Benjamin looked over at her with pride at how composed she remained throughout all the questioning. He had Captain Gordon send her uniform to her and she looked very professional. He knew this was all a formality but it was necessary to rule out any unethical action.

An officer of the court entered the room with a sheet of paper in his hand interrupting the private discussion of the three men.

Benjamin and JC exchanged glances wondering what it could be.

After reading the paper, the three men nodded and the District Attorney handed the paper to the court stenographer.

JC and Benjamin stood up as the District Attorney approached them.

He had a huge smile on his face, "Officer Smith and Mr. Murphy, you are free to go. Mr. Lentz has pleaded guilty. There will be no trial." He put forth his hand to shake JC's, "Officer Smith, I personally want to thank you for performing your duty. Your action in my estimation probably saved more injuries or even a life if Mr. Lentz had not been stopped."

Turning to shake Benjamin's hand, "And you Sir, I'm glad to see you healing and I hope this doesn't sour you on helping the less fortunate with free advice in the future. I look forward to seeing you in court again." His phone rang and he excused himself.

The other two men smiled, picked up their brief cases and said good-bye. To them it was just another busy day in the life of law enforcement.

JC sat back down relieved that the hearing was over. Benjamin joined her.

"What's the matter, you okay?" He took her hand in his.

"Yeah I was just thinking that in all the years grandpa was the sheriff, he never had to shoot anyone. He always managed to talk people into putting down their weapon. It was usually someone who had too much to drink. He'd put them in jail overnight, give them a fine for disorderly conduct and let the wife or mother give them the rest of the sentence. You might say it was our version 'Mayberry'. I'm in town for two days and I shoot a man." She looked over at him, "And the worse thing is, I wonder what I'd do if that one bullet had been a fatal one."

Benjamin took her in his arms and rested his chin on her head. "My dear, you would have done exactly what you did. You are a police officer who knows her duty, and you are a Christian woman who doesn't go by the idea of 'an eye for an eye' theory. You followed the law. In addition, remember, this man wasn't going to listen to you. Had you walked toward him, I have no doubt the first bullet would have went to you." He stood up and offered her his hand. "Now, I don't know about you, but I'm hungry. I bet George waiting outside is hungry. I think we need to celebrate by getting a super duper hot dog with all the trimming from a side walk vendor."

Slowly she stood up smiling, put her arms around his waist, and hugged him tight. "Right you are counselor. Off to get one of New York's finest."

Hand and hand, they slowly ambled out of the room, with a sense of peace that this whole mess was behind them.

JC didn't say anything to Benjamin as they quietly left the building, but she had to go home and she wanted to return. She knew he wanted her to stay longer, but she needed to see how bad her house was. Hopefully, he could go back with her. She didn't want to fly back alone and she wanted him by her as they dealt with the other mess caused by Tim.

* * *

"You want me to go back to Freedomville with you, why?" Betty had a look of surprise on her face. "What would I possible have to do there?" She paused pointing a finger at them, "Are you two planning on a small country wedding on the sly?"

Benjamin laughed, "I wish that was why."

"Actually," JC put her hand on Betty's arm, "We want you as a chaperone. If my home is in such a trashed state, I can't stay there and…" she looked at Benjamin, "even though I am the present owner of the mansion, Benjamin has been calling it home. He needs a place to stay too and you know how small towns can gossip. Yes, I could stay with Harold's family or my friends, but…" her voice trailed off.

Betty waved her hands in the air, "Okay, okay, what time do we leave, how long will I be there, what kind of clothes do I need to pack, and oh yes, we will have to let security here know how we can be reached."

In a serious tone Benjamin answered her. "Betty, we don't know. I feel I need to be by JC's side as she has decisions to make. The law firm will fax me as before, and you can call anyone or get on the internet you know. The town is civilized. There are a couple of motels in town, but you will fall in love with the mansion and there are many comfortable bedrooms. I took grandfather's room when I was there. It's up to JC where she wants us now." Smiling he put his arm around her.

"Bring whatever you will be comfortable in. If you are there until Sunday and wish to join us for church, most of the women wear dresses. We do have a couple of nice restaurants you might want to wear something besides jeans. There are bikes, horses to ride on the farm, walking trails, a small golf course on the edge of town, flowers to pick, the whole third floor full of history and there is plenty of places to fish." JC spoke in an excited voice; her face was animated as she listed the activities available.

Wrapping both arms around him, "Benjamin, you might be interested in going through the old safe more thoroughly. I'm sure there is more of your grandfather you can learn from going through the rest of the things. Besides you know anything you want that is in the mansion is yours. Your very unselfish gift to me..," she slowly turned her head side to side fighting back tears, "We share it, and if I remember correctly, one said Benjamin," she waved her left hand with the engagement ring on it, "asked me to marry him. And, unless he wants to take back that question due to the shock of his injury, I would say that it is both of ours." She burst out laughing.

"Don't think you can get out of your answer of yes. I'm a very important attorney you know." Benjamin picked her up and swirled her around.

"Okay you two." Betty was laughing but trying to look stern, "What time do we leave tomorrow and who is interested in the casserole resting in the oven that is probably all dried out by now?"

Putting an arm around the waist of both women, as the three walked down the hall toward the kitchen, Benjamin said, "I'll call the pilots, do you think about ten is okay."

The women looked at each other and nodded yes.

"Okay, JC if you will call Harold and let them know so they stock up the refrigerator at the mansion, oops, I guess that decision is yours to make." He smiled at her.

"Betty, you let security know here and your friends, I'll leave word at the office, and let's eat. That hotdog for lunch wasn't very filling and I'm starved."

As they each fixed their plates and carried them to the table, JC asked, "What if we go food shopping ourselves when we get back? Betty can see our town, the two groceries stores and if we don't feel like cooking, there are always grilled cheese sandwiches or scrambled eggs."

Benjamin pointed the knife he was using to butter his bread at Betty, "JC mentioned those two meals because the only other food she prepares is bagels and cheese or fish and corn on the cob baked in a campfire, which I haven't eaten yet, but she tells me she does a superb job of."

"Or we could order in pizza, which is what Benjamin usually offers as a choice when I was slaving away helping him." Everyone burst out laughing.

"On the safe side, I think I'll pack the picnic basket. There is ham and fresh veggies that will go bad if we leave them here. That should take care of our supper the first night." Betty looked at them both for an okay.

"Okay. They both said as one.

Twirling her fork around in the casserole, JC asked quietly, "Should I pack all the lovely dresses or leave them here. I don't have anything to put them in."

Betty and Benjamin exchanged glances, and then Betty spoke for both of them. "Perhaps if you chose one that you would wear first at the mansion, say at an engagement party, and leave the others here for flying back with Benjamin for shows, dinners and things like that. I have a garment bag you can use."

"That sounds logical to me. I wish the beautiful blue dress wasn't stained with blood. I felt like a princess that night in it." JC eyes were sad, "But, I'm so thankful you weren't killed."

"My dear, you look beautiful to me when you wear jeans, your uniform, anything."

"Ahem, will the mutual admiration society pause a moment, anyone want dessert?" Betty's eyes twinkled but mentally she was so glad the couple was so open around her.

"None for me thank you. I need to phone Harold so he can meet us with the car and also call the captain and see when he wants me to come back to work. And then I need to work out or I'll have to let this uniform out at the seams." JC laughed as she stood up and puffed out her cheeks.

Speaking in a low voice, Benjamin suggested, "I wouldn't be too hasty in calling the captain yet. First wait and see what the house looks like, get some clothes over to the mansion and settled in, things like that. Yes, when you get back give him a jingle, but you still need some time off to deal with everything. I could do that for you, but I know as independent as you are, you'll want to do it. And we need to go see how John is doing at home."

"You're correct, Benjamin. I'm not use to having someone share my decision making, especially after Grandpa and Mr.

Murphy passed away. Thanks." She leaned down and kissed him gently on the lips.

Betty began picking up the dishes, "I think I heard JC mention working out, Benjie you better call the head pilot and the office, then start packing. I'll load the dishwasher and pack. Oh, do I need to bring any books to read?"

Benjamin and JC broke out laughing. "You should see the library at the mansion and there is one in town, and if I remember correctly, didn't I give you a Nook for Christmas?" Benjamin raised his right eyebrow.

Again, seeing him do that reminded her of how many mannerisms Benjamin had that was like his grandfather.

"Okay, shoo, you two, we all have things to do." Betty waved them away. As she bent to put the soap into the dishwasher, she mused, *it's a good thing I'm going with them after all, to see how things are there. It just seems likes this passion Benjie has for JC and the engagement came so fast, and then to give her the property.* She stood up and stared into space. *I want what is best for Benjie and I pray this is genuine between them and he won't get hurt. He has lost so much. This should be a very interesting trip.*

CHAPTER TWENTY

Craig Rowley, a fellow reporter whose beat was informing the public about interesting court proceedings, perched on the corner of Mike's desk. "Remember that small town lady cop, the friend of the big shot lawyer? Well," he consulted his notes, "That Lentz guy she shot pleaded guilty; she is off the hook and free to go home." He pointed at the news clipping of her Mike had under the glass on his desk, remarking in a ribbing way, "I don't think you'll be having any more dances with her."

Quickly Mike slid some papers over the picture as he snapped back, "I just kept that article because I was interested in the outcome of the case, nothing more." Leaning back against his leather chair, "I will admit she sure was one looker, and that perfume she wore was very sexy."

Craig peered over at the wastepaper basket, "Yeah, right, you've been on a diet ever since that night. I remember over hearing you tell the guys you referred to her as a hottie and wondered if there were more like her at home. You honestly think you can compete with that money pockets lawyer. All dames want money. Hey you got some big bucks hidden?" Craig snickered.

"Don't read anything in my trying to lose some weight. The seat belts are getting a little snug, that's all, I gotta do something." Mike smiled waving him off his desk, "Now get going, I've got to write up a column on the big doings going on at the country club… some of us have exciting news people want to read, especially if their name is in it."

Watching Craig walk away, the smile left Mike's face. *That was a little too close to the truth. If he could lose weight, he might have a chance with Miss Janice Caroline Smith. He liked the sound of her name.* He remembered how she felt that short time in his arms. Um, nice! Her soft yet firm body, not all flabby or encased in those female undergarments some wore to make themselves look fit. Imagining how she would feel with nothing on at all, he groaned softly envisioning it in his mind.

Mike quickly sat straight up and looked around. He had to watch his emotions. Craig already was smarting off.

Reaching into his pocket for his notebook, he flipped it open amazed at how easy it was to get her home address.

Unzipping his briefcase, he retrieved a Hallmark card with roses on the front then began typing on his computer.

> Roses pale next to your beauty
> Your face softer than their pedals
> I worship you from afar
> My beauty.

Placing the blank page on the printer, he hit print. Picking up the card he reread it, yes his sentiments exactly. Putting the envelope in the printer, he addressed it then pressed a stamp on it making sure it was secure and slid it back into his briefcase. Later he would drop it into a mailbox where he wouldn't be seen. He didn't want anyone to observe him mailing anything because he usually put all his mail in the out box for the office boy to collect.

Glancing at the time, he deleted the message and address, shut down his computer and made sure nothing was left for prying eyes. Picking up his briefcase, he wondered if the exercise machine he ordered was delivered to his apartment today. He had left word with the doorman to let them in and have them assemble it. He was too embarrassed to go to a gym yet to work out.

His stomach growled letting him know the small salad he had for lunch wasn't enough. A steak and a strong whiskey would be nice, then JC's sexy body came to mind, and he shook his head, no! The whiskey had calories in it and so would the marbled prime rib steak he usually ordered. He sighed, guess he'd stop and pick up one of those frozen diet food meals that tasted like the container it was in and another readymade salad. She would be worth it. Taking a swig of water, he capped the bottle and slid it in his briefcase. How long would it take to lose enough weight so he could approach her, let her see he was what she needed? There was no denying he wanted her, bad.

CHAPTER TWENTY-ONE

JC pulled into the driveway and turned off the ignition. She couldn't believe there was a yellow ribbon all around her home saying 'caution, do not to enter'. Turning to look at Benjamin and Betty, "This sign says a lot. I didn't believe Harold when he said the house had to be demolished and he began to cry. I thought he was so emotional and embarrassed because Tim is his son and responsible for the damage."

They all got out of the Jeep, ducked under the ribbon, and approached the house.

She didn't have to worry about unlocking the door; it had been smashed with probably a sledge hammer. Taking one finger she pushed at what was left of it and it opened to the kitchen in shambles. She inhaled sharply. "Oh no! I can't believe Tim would do this much destruction."

Benjamin put his arms around her. Betty stared in disbelief. Tim had used an axe on the walls and counter, pulled the refrigerator over, and threw dishes on the floor. It was a mess. JC never said a word as they carefully walked through the broken dishes, cans of food mixed with flour and sugar thrown on the floor and went into the living room.

More chaos. JC knelt down and carefully picked up a shattered picture of her parents, and next to it, one of her grandparents who raised her. She stayed there in the crouched position as tears ran down her face.

Benjamin leaned down and gently pulled her to her feet and held her close as she sobbed into his chest.

Betty picked up some pictures of JC with her grandfather and a few with Mr. Murphy, well she assumed it was Mr. Murphy. The man looked like William and Benjie.

Composing herself, JC left the comfort of Benjamin's arms, looked around her, waded through the mounds of the torn up davenport cushions, chairs, the smashed TV, lamps, and windows, and with a shocked look on her face entered the bedroom. Her closet was bare of clothes; they were all ripped up and thrown on the bed that he had used the axe to chop up.

Shaking her head with disbelief, she stepped over torn clothes to the bathroom. The first thing that got her attention was the message in lipstick written on the wall, 'If I can't have you, no one will.'

Her balled up fist was against her mouth as she moaned out, "Oh no!"

Benjamin's jaw was set tight with anger. Those words could stand up in court as a threat to her life. Tenderly, he took her arm and led her out of the trashed room. "Let's go home Honey to the mansion, there is nothing to be salvaged here."

Betty nodded at Benjamin. He was right and JC needed to get away from all of the destruction and memories and shock that someone she grew up with could be so malicious. They were all silent as once again they retraced their steps carefully through the living room, glass crunching beneath their feet. Betty stooped to pick up four of the pictures that only the glass was broken. She would have them reframed for JC. Maybe they could find some albums later that hadn't been destroyed. Her heart went out for the girl. At least JC had Benjamin to be with her to navigate through the legal aspect this mess would bring. She worried that JC was in shock since she didn't scream, shout or comment on anything. It was as if something inside her had died.

* * *

Outside, JC took a deep breath and slowly looked around at her surroundings. She had always felt safe here. It was only recently she even locked the doors. But now, she felt violated, her security and trust shaken.

"Give me the Jeep keys, JC. I'm driving." Benjamin held out his hand.

As JC handed him the keys, Benjamin noticed her eyes had hardened, she stood straighter. He had never witnessed her like this.

"Before we go to the mansion, I want to talk with the captain."

With a low soft voice Benjamin asked, "Do you really want to do this now? All of this has been quite a shock."

In a cold monotone voice, "I need to know everything, Benjamin; you saw how upset Harold was to the point he had one of the farm hands drive us to the mansion. Don't you understand, I need to talk with the captain and see if he knows more about this?" Her voice rose as she spoke the last part of the sentence, she was very close to losing it.

"Yes, my dear, I understand, I want to know also. I'm surprised the captain didn't call you and be more specific before we came back." He opened the Jeep door, folded down the seat for Betty to get in and put it back so JC could enter.

* * *

The three sat on the opposite side of the desk listening as the captain calmly told them what had transpired. It didn't take a brain surgeon to see JC was hanging on her emotions by a thread.

"Harold thought Tim had just slipped out of the evaluation/ detox center. Actually, he knocked out one of the nurses, breaking her nose in the process, and pulled her badge off to swipe out of the building, tearing her uniform in the process. From there he broke into a bar, grabbed a bottle of whiskey and checked the street for any cars with the keys in them. You know this town; many leave them in the vehicle. Then he drove to your place and started to drink. He retrieved your sledgehammer and axe from your unlocked shed, and that led to all the damage.

Curt, who was on the night patrol, noticed the lights on at your place and investigated knowing you were out of town, and called for assistance; Tim was one nasty drunk and waving the axe around." He sighed. I'm glad you weren't home at the time, JC. The judge has Tim put in the mental health ward for evaluation to see if he is mentally stable to be charged. I know how hard all of this has been for you."

"Captain," JC's voice was so low, it was hard to hear her, "I need some more time off. I'm a bit upset right now; I guess I'm not as strong as I thought I was." Her face was ashen, her eyes wide with fear, "What would have happened if I had been home when he came with that sledge hammer and axe. What would I have had to do to stop him? Shoot him? I've known him all my life!" She shuddered and began to cry.

Immediately both men went to her, Betty handed her a tissue.

Kneeling down by her, the Captain put his hand on her knee, "JC, take all the time you need. This has been a shock, you aren't weak, I would feel the same if that had been my home." He hugged her. "I've known you all your life, you've come through a lot, and trust me, you will make it though this like a champion. You're a Smith, remember?"

Looking over at Benjamin, "Take her home, do you want me to call the doc about a sedative?"

Benjamin shook his head no, "I think Betty and I will take care of her. I'll call the doctor or take her to the hospital if we deem it necessary. Betty can assist her in a warm bath, a back rub and some warm relaxing tea. I think the scope of what has transpired and what could have happened has hit her. We will talk it out with her after she has some rest. Trust me; we will take very good care of her."

The captain could see the devotion that Mr. Murphy displayed; it reminded him of Benjamin's grandfather, he also noticed the huge ring on JC's finger. He stood up nodding at him, "I'll see you out. Call me if you need anything at all."

He watched as the two people one on each side of JC, walked her to the Jeep. The lady Betty impressed him with her kind nature. Smiling to himself, he had a feeling he might be looking for another police officer in the near future. He also wanted a chat with Mr. Jensen.

* * *

Betty walked into the study, rubbing her lower back. "She's asleep. The bath and back rub helped, so did the cup of mint tea. She is wearing one of my nightgowns. I think I'll wash up and sit in the chair tonight in case she wakes up."

"I'll keep you company. I vacillate from angry to sad. I feel so frustrated that I can't take away the pain and I didn't see this coming. I should have been more diligent after his other attempt to break into her house. We just thought it was the actions of a drunk." Benjamin ran his hand through his hair. "Tomorrow I want to have another talk with Harold, and see how John is doing. He is a tough old bird and I'm sure will have some input on this situation. We need to get her some more clothes too. Do you think you should go get a few things for her until she is ready to face people and their questions, or should I just call The House of Cheree's and have her send out things to pick from?"

Betty put her hand on his arm, "Let's see how she is after a good night's sleep. I don't have her pegged as one to stay down very long and it might be a nice diversion to go look for some clothes, but maybe not in this town. Now, if you're going to keep me company in her room, let's get into something comfortable and grab a blanket and pillow. I don't know about you but I am thoroughly exhausted."

"I'm so glad you are here." Benjamin put his arms around Betty giving her a warm hug. "What would I do without you?"

* * *

JC awoke with a start from the huge clock in the hallway chiming out the hour. Lying back against the pillows it took her a moment to remember that she was in the room she always stayed in when she was at the mansion. The mansion! She sat straight up. Her mansion, no, her home, her new home, her home was trashed, by Tim. Unbelievable.

Sighing, she swung her feet to the side of the bed, surprised to see she was wearing a nightgown. She always wore pajamas; this must be one of Betty's. Making a gentle fist, JC rubbed the sleep from her eyes and sighed. Last night was such a blur. She had felt disbelief, anger, loss and fear. Well, that was last night and today was a new day. It was time to get up, she had decisions to make. Walking over to the closet, she opened the door to see if there were any of her clothes left there from when Willard was ill. There were, good, no one threw them out. Taking a pair of jeans, she went over to the dresser and she took out a tee-shirt and some underwear.

Just as she was going to take a shower, a soft tapping on the door stopped her.

"JC? Are you awake, Honey?" Benjamin's voice was soft.

"Yes, come in."

Opening the door, Benjamin was surprised to see her standing in the middle of the room with clothes over her arm. She looked tired, but not in shock for which he was grateful.

"Betty made some coffee and I have a cup here for you if you like. Where did you get the clothes?"

"Coffee, um, sounds good. My clothes were in the closet from when I stayed here when your grandfather was ill. I got busy and forgot about them, and the help left everything. I'm surprised, because we boxed up your grandfather's things and put them in the attic."

Benjamin turned and picked up the tray from the table outside her room and put it on the round table by the window. Then he poured the fragrant coffee into the mug from the carafe and added some creamer, stirred it with a spoon and handed it to her.

"Thank you, Benjamin, I'd give you a kiss, but I haven't brushed my teeth yet." She smiled at him and took a sip of the coffee. "Um."

Leaning down, Benjamin kissed her lightly on the lips. "Let's start over. Good morning, Beautiful."

She kissed him back, "Good morning."

"If the mutual admiration society is done, I'm here to say breakfast will be ready in fifteen minutes. Where did those clothes from?" Betty voice showed she was surprised.

"My closet. Give me time to hop in the shower and I'll be there in time for breakfast, for some reason, I'm famished." JC took another sip of coffee and opened the bathroom door, "Fifteen minutes on the dot."

Betty and Benjamin shared a look between them and left the room.

"I was surprised to see her so upbeat. I was sure she would be in a depressed mood considering how things were last night. I found it odd too that she didn't have any nightmares." Betty picked up the tray.

Benjamin nodded his head, "She is a pretty resilient person. Perhaps the care we gave her last night helped. You see why I'm so crazy about her? Most women would have been a basket case today." He stopped and looked at Betty, "You two have so much in common, I'm one lucky man to have you both in my life. Now, what can I do to help with breakfast?"

Laughing she responded, "You set the table, I'm still finding my way around the kitchen."

As they entered the kitchen, the phone rang.

CHAPTER TWENTY-TWO

Harold stood with the phone against his ear.

"Did they answer yet?" John leaned forward, his elbows on the table, anxious like a kid waiting for Christmas.

Harold waved his hand at his dad to hush. "Good morning, Benjamin. Harold here. At the council meeting last night, the captain took me aside and told me how upset our JC was after seeing her home. Dad and I would like to come over and talk with her," he paused and his voice lowered, "If you think it would be okay and not upset her more."

Benjamin was surprised in away with the call, but understood the concern they had for JC. "We are about to have breakfast. JC is in the shower now. She was really shook up yesterday; I don't think any of us thought the damage to the house would be that extensive. It came as a severe shock to her. After a good night's sleep, she was in a positive mood when Betty and I went to take her some coffee this morning. What if we drive over to your place and not inconvenience John. How is he doing by the way?"

Smiling at his dad, Harold responded, "Dad is doing great and worried about JC. Not to see her would cause him stress."

"JC just came into the kitchen, let me ask her. One moment please." Benjamin put his hand over the receiver. "Harold is on the line. He and John would like to come over and talk with you. I suggested we could go there because of John recovering, but John would like to come here. What do you want?"

"Here is fine." She pointed at the clock, smiled and mouthed 'fifteen minutes'.

Removing his hand from the phone, Benjamin spoke, "JC says here is fine, give us time to eat unless you want to join us."

Laughing Harold responded, "Thanks, but we ate about an hour ago, you know what an early riser dad is. We'll see you in about forty-five minutes if that's okay."

"Fine, see you then." They both hung up.

Benjamin looked at both of the ladies watching him, "They will be here by the time we are done eating. They both are feeling terrible about what happened and need to see you." He kissed JC on the lips. "Um, you brushed your teeth." They both laughed.

The toaster made the pop sound signifying the toast was up; Betty began to butter the two slices. "Now, if it wouldn't be too much of an imposition, would one of you dish up the scrambled eggs and put the fruit on the table."

They sat down and joined hands with JC offering the blessing over the food and for peace of mind.

"Last night after you fell to sleep, Benjamin and I were discussing your need for a new wardrobe. I know you will have to order your uniforms for work, but would you like to go shopping in town, another town, or have The House of Cheree's Boutique sent out a selection?"

Her fork midway to her mouth JC looked surprised, "Cheree's Boutique? Here? They don't handle the type of clothes I normally wear."

"She has another outlet in town by a different name. I can have a selection flown here by this afternoon." Benjamin took a bite of his toast. "And, if you don't want to go back to work," he looked tenderly at her, "We could get married and you wouldn't need the uniforms and you could help me set up a Murphy Foundation or be involved in doing community work here or whatever you would be interested in, like raising some little Murphys."

JC looked back and forth at Benjamin and Betty, blushing at what Benjamin had just said. So many thoughts were going through her mind, shooting Mr. Lentz, her trashed home, Benjamin, marriage. Everything was moving too fast.

They were interrupted by a knock on the door.

Benjamin went to open it even though this was now JC's place.

"Good morning, come in," he shook John's hand and then Harold's, noticing that John was moving slow but okay and his color was good. Harold's face was one of a troubled man.

As the two men entered the kitchen, JC flew around the table and threw her arms around them both and they hugged. Tears from John's eyes slowly trickled down his wrinkled checks, while Harold pulled out a large white handkerchief and loudly blew his nose.

John took JC by her arms and held her back and looked her over. "How you doin' little gal?"

"I'm doing fine, John, how about you? The doc give you the okay to gallivant around?" She closed up the space between them and hugged him again. "I'm so glad to see you again."

Patting her gently on the back, "And me you. Could I sit down now?"

"Yes, yes, here, take my chair." JC pulled it back from the table.

Benjamin got up from his and said to Harold, "Take mine, would you both like some coffee or juice?"

The men declined.

"Would you two like to talk with JC alone?" Benjamin asked looking at the men. He realized while she was like a daughter to them he was still a stranger.

"No." JC answered for them. "John, Harold, Benjamin proposed to me, and I feel anything that needs to be said should be with all of us," she looked over at Betty including her. "We are family, right?"

A huge smile came over John and Harold. "We weren't surprised to hear that since the captain said he saw this big rock on your finger and he didn't think it came from a Cracker Jack box. Congratulations!"

Harold pumped Benjamin's hand and up and down then hugged JC. "Encase you're interested, dad and I think this is good news. Have you two set a date yet?"

"No." JC smiled.

"Soon I hope," Benjamin put his arm around her, "I love her very much."

"I always say, if you know it's right, there's no reason to wait. My dear wife and I didn't wait and we had a good long marriage."

"Now, we came over to see what we can do to replace your house. It broke my heart to see how my son could do such a thing to you. He is getting mental help now. They told me not to come and see him for awhile; they will let me know when." Harold hung his head.

"Just a minute, I'll be right back." JC quickly left the room and returned shortly with the blood stained envelope. Removing the two deeds, she handed them to John who passed them to Harold.

John looked up at Benjamin; then he arose from his chair and walked over to Benjamin first extending his hand, then gave him a manly hug. "You truly are Willard's grandson. That is something he would do. Was this a marriage present?"

"No. Not a present, not a bribe to marry me, just to give her peace of mind. She loves this place as well you know. I don't have the warm memories she does, and this is hers free and clear and as you read, so is the farm surrounding it. When we get married, this will be our home here and I have one in New York. We have many plans to make."

JC spoke up, "When I woke up this morning, I had an idea I would like to bounce off all of you." Her glance included everyone in the room. "With the insurance money from the house, I was wondering if we couldn't build a half way house for those like Tim that have alcohol or mental problems to make a transition into the main stream of life. I realize I would need to check on the zoning, work with the town council and the medical establishment. We could also incorporate the ladies aid at church to maybe teach cooking skills or provide some homemaking classes and management of finances. I know many would need some job skills; we could have the computer classes and so forth. I can see a basketball hoop put out side. What do you think?"

Surprised, they all looked at her.

"Are you sure? What about your job? This is an undertaking of large proportions." Betty was the first to speak up.

"When," JC gave a warm smile to Benjamin, "When we get married, Benjamin suggested I might want to leave the police force. He has such a thriving business in New York and we will be traveling back and forth, and he also suggested this morning he would like to start a foundation or something similar that I would be involved in." Her voice got quiet, "Shooting that man...I'm so glad I didn't have to kill him, but...I think maybe I'm not cut out for that job anymore."

Old John slowly got up from the chair, "This is all great news, and it warms my heart. I would like to be part of it. For now, I need to go home and rest a bit. Will the wedding be here at the mansion, the church or New York?"

JC and Benjamin exchanged glances, "We don't know yet, we haven't set a date even. You will be the first to know." She kissed him on the check, "And you will walk me down the aisle where ever it is."

"And I will be honored to do so." John's face was wreathed in a smile.

"Well Dad, we better leave now so you can get rested up." Harold touched his dad's elbow. "And you two call me for anything, anytime, that's what family is for you know."

Benjamin walked with the two men out to the truck.

"You're a good man, Benjamin." John remarked as Benjamin helped him up into the truck.

Benjamin stepped away and watched as the truck went down the road.

Wedding, the law firm, JC's plans… they had better get busy doing some planning, oh yes, and JC needs a wardrobe. He quickly headed toward the house. Married was top of his list.

CHAPTER TWENTY-THREE

The warmth of the sun felt good as JC walked down the long driveway to see if there was any mail in the mailbox, an exact replica of the mansion. She smiled, remembering how she helped paint it one summer.

She had the mail forward to the mansion after hearing about her trashed home. If they ever put in sidewalks, she knew the rural mail delivery would be over. Times were changing. The council meeting was the second Thursday of every month; she usually went when she wasn't on duty. They would be the ones to make that decision… the tax payers might object to an increase in property taxes. Oh well, time would tell, not to worry.

Pulling down the lid of the large box, she retrieved a handful of mail. Quickly glancing through it all she noticed a one card with her full name on it but no return address. Um. Retracing her steps, she just enjoyed the freedom of being outside. Reaching the porch, she sat down in a chair and began opening the mail. There were the usual bills and junk mail. Picking up the card, she turned it over, no address on the back either but noticed it was postmarked from New York. Carefully sliding her finger under the flap to open it, she pulled out the card. *Um, pretty roses on the front.* Opening it up she read the verse. *No signature. Weird.*

As JC walked into the house she called out, "Benjamin, where are you?"

"In the office, slaving away."

Entering the room, JC placed the card on the desk. "Did you send this and forget to sign it?"

Picking up the card, Benjamin swiftly read the verse and shook his head. "No, it's not from me, I at least can rhyme. Wasn't there a return address?"

"No." She handed him the envelope. "You don't think this was from Tim do you?"

"From the stamped date here, that would have been after Tim was arrested," he looked up at her, "You have no idea who might have sent it?"

"No, the police and ER have my address, but no one else. I realize you can go on the internet and find most anything, but I don't even know anyone in New York to give them my address."

"There is no way anyone would have mailed out anything from Tim, especially to arrange this. I think you might have a secret admirer. It worries me though. I think we should share this with the Captain Gordon." Benjamin's face was somber. "I must say I don't like this and think it would be wise if you have someone with you at all times until we find out who this mysterious person is."

"Aren't you over reacting about this Benjamin, it's only a card?" JC circled the desk and placed her hands on his shoulders resting her chin on his head.

Reaching up and taking her hands in his, he quietly remarked, "We didn't over react to Tim's attempt to break into your home and look what happened." He got out of his chair and took her in his arms. "Would you understand if I said I have that gut feeling? I could never forgive myself if I let anything happen to you. Someone sent that card, it wasn't me. We need to think back about who I introduced you to in New York. Or" he paused, "it could be some kook who read about the shooting in the paper. I'm going to call the office and see if anyone inquired about you or your address. We need to take this to the captain too. I'm sure there won't be any fingers prints with all the handling, but it's worth a try."

Walking into the room, "Hey you two, I thought we were going shopping and here you are playing huggy." Betty stopped at the serious look on both of their faces. "What's the matter, are you okay, JC?"

Handing her the card, Benjamin asked, "Have you seen this before?"

"No. And it's not signed. Why the question?" Betty handed it back.

"I didn't send it, you didn't, and it was mailed from New York. Whom does JC know there but you, me and George? We are going to take it into town and show it to the captain."

JC took Betty's hand. "Don't worry; it's probably someone's idea of a joke to make Benjamin jealous. We'll stop and show the captain and then go shopping." JC smiled but inside she was worried. *With all her training, she knew about stalkers. Sure, they might be over reacting, but...* She shivered remembering her trashed home.

* * *

Captain Gordon leaned back in his chair, "It's amazing what tests can do, but I'm on the same page as Benjamin, there may not be any fingerprints on this, but we will check. We have JC's on file; let's get Benjamin's and Betty's. We can see about the type of print on the card, not sure anything will come of it, but it won't hurt to try. Do you want me to assign someone to watch the mansion?"

"No thanks, I don't think that will be necessary since it is wired with the silent alarm. JC is here, we will notify Harold and John to be more on a look out and... I didn't tell you but I am licensed for conceal carry in New York, but my gun is back there. I have also taken some self-defense courses. I think it's best that JC is always with someone." Benjamin looked over at Betty, "And Betty has a belt in Karate."

JC did a double take; *she never expected that of Benjamin or Betty.*

Betty smiled, "One needs to be prepared for the unknown on the streets of New York."

Resting his arms on the desk the captain asked Benjamin, "This fellow in New York who shot you, think he might want to cause you some mental distress?"

Benjamin shook his head, "He doesn't strike me as one who can navigate around the internet to find JC's address. He might be able to tell us what street corner a dealer would have some drugs, nah. But, he would have privileges for the computer at the prison, but he would need someone to purchase a card and mail it out. If it came from the prison, it would be postmarked."

"JC, I want you to be careful, hear me? I've known you all your life and you are like one of my own," the captain came around his desk and gave her a hug. "I know you are bothered by shooting that man. You still need to come in for those counseling sessions for situations like this. In the meantime, carry your weapon with you, just to be safe."

"Okay, captain. Today I need to get some needed clothes. I'll be safe having my two trusty body guards with me, Kunfoo Betty and Dead-eye Benjamin."

They all laughed. But Captain Gordon thought that pretty, Ms Betty was to dainty to have a belt in martial arts.

Benjamin was going to make a call; he would have twenty-four hour bodyguards flown in, today. He would do that while he waited as the women tried on clothes. No one was going to mess with his lady.

CHAPTER TWENTY-FOUR

"I still don't know why you didn't want us to use the Jeep?" JC looked over at Benjamin.

"Well, I think the Explorer needs to be driven too. I'm surprised Granddad didn't have all the vehicles sold. Besides, we need enough room for all the shopping you ladies will be doing. I could use a few more things also." *And I think this is safer with the tinted windows if there is someone out there watching JC.*

Laughing JC looked over at Betty, "It's a good thing we had a hearty breakfast, shopping is such hard work. I was worn out after trying on all those gowns in New York. At least all I need is comfy clothes and a couple of dresses, oh yes, some shoes and a few pieces of jewelry. Bet we can make it one stop shopping."

"You're kidding, right? Everything from undies to church clothes in one store?" Betty caught Benjamin's glance through the mirror. This was a small town.

"Well almost. Benjamin, you can find a parking spot anywhere now. Oh look at those bridal gowns; I know where to come when we set a date." JC kept her eyes on the window as Benjamin parked the vehicle.

"You can't get that dress today because Benjie isn't supposed to see the gown until the day of the wedding." Betty unhooked her seatbelt.

"I'll close my eyes while you pick one out." Benjamin replied, "I want to call JC my wife as soon as possible. She can wear Levi's if she wants too." He opened his door, then came around and opened the doors for the two women. "Which shop first, JC?"

"The one next to the bridal shop has nice dress up clothes. Across the street," she pointed, "They carry shoes. Up two blocks is more of a sport shop where I can get workout clothes. Then if we stop at the big box store, I can purchase undergarments. I can also pick up some earrings. Then, I shall be all ready for a big lunch at the Mexican Cafe...you're buying lunch of course." She kissed him.

"Of course. Um is this my practice for the roll of hubby?"

"Ahuh. You have to take George's place today. Remember how he said we were running out of room in the limo?" JC patted the side of the Explorer, "We can always pile things on top with tie downs." They all smiled at that remark.

Betty interjected, "Or we could have them delivered if we really want to shop. Plus we don't have to do it all in one day you know; I think I heard you say mention lunch later."

As they entered the small shop, the bell over the door gave a friendly jingle.

An elderly lady dressed professionally came forward with her arms open. "How nice to see you JC." She enveloped her in a warm hug. "I haven't seen you in church lately. I heard you were out of town and..." she lowered her voice looking at Benjamin and Betty, "and what happened to your home. I'm so sorry."

"Thank you Ms Rose. I want you to meet my future husband, Benjamin Murphy and a very dear friend, Betty. We are here to get some of your beautiful clothes I can wear for church."

Ms Rose looked at JC, "Come with me, I just got a new shipment in and I have some that will be perfect with your coloring." She linked her arm with JC's.

"Betty, come with me, I need you input too you know," JC smiled at Betty.

Benjamin sat down, "I'll just keep company with this chair while you ladies shop." As soon as they were out of hearing, Benjamin punched in the numbers to his office. "Good morning to you, Susan. Put me through to Sam please."

"Sam speaking."

"Sam, Benjamin here. You haven't had anyone calling to inquire about JC have you?"

"No, Benjamin. Why do you ask?"

"Just curious, she got some mail that wasn't signed. Remember those bodyguards we hired for the Kingston case, I want you to get those same four men and have them flown out on my plane as soon as possible. I don't want anyone else to know they are coming but me. If need be they can call me to negotiate the salary and time frame, otherwise, the current rate they charged before. Let me know when they are coming so I can pick them up at the airport. Oh, and call The House of Cherri's Boutique and have them make another blue dress the exact duplicate as the one that got blood all over it and mail it to my address here in Freedomville. She will know which one, they don't mass produce her dresses and JC's picture was in the paper with the messed up dress. I'll check the fax when I get back to the mansion about any office questions or comments."

They discussed a few business details when Benjamin heard the dressing room door open, "Gotta go, later," and clicked his phone off.

All three ladies were smiling as they brought their arms full of clothes to the counter.

Standing up Benjamin joined them. "Are you sure you have enough here?"

"Well, I'm also purchasing a few things, I love this shop." Betty placed her selection down next to JC's dresses, skirts, blouses and two sweaters and jacket.

"Why don't we look for shoes now while Ms Rose totals the purchases and wraps them up." He leaned over to Ms Rose speaking low, "Put them all on one bill and select some jewelry to go with these lovely selections JC chose." He gave her a big smile. "I'll be back to pay for them."

"Of course, Mr. Murphy."

"Call me Benjamin, Ms Rose.

"Benjamin." She liked him more and more. JC really filled her in how wonderful he was. A regular a chip off the Willard Murphy block, his granddad was always picking up the tab for others too.

Three more shops and the ladies had crossed off their list the items JC needed. It would have gone quicker but they were constantly running into friends and acquaintances of JC. As the women placed those purchases in the vehicle, Benjamin went inside the dress shop, paid the bill and made the first of two trips, his arms loaded with the boxes of gently folded clothes.

"Thanks, Honey for bringing those out, I'll go in and pay for them." JC gave him a gentle squeeze on his arm.

"I took care of that, JC."

With a quiet yet stern voice, "Benjamin, I have money, you don't have to buy my clothes." JC stood with one hand on her hip.

"I wanted to and I paid for Betty's too. Besides, what difference does it make who pays for them? Hopefully we will be married soon and what's mine is yours etc." He smiled. "Now, I'm famished from all this shopping, I think you mentioned a Mexican place to eat."

JC hesitated for a minute; she didn't want Ms Rose to think she was one of those rich man's girlfriend. "Café. Mexican Café." She kissed her fingers and waved them in the air.

"What those yummy hot dogs sold from the sidewalk vendors were in New York, this is the country equivalent."

After lunch, on the ride back home, JC rested her head against the seat. She was tired, not only the shopping and decisions, but also the reason for needing the clothes. Once they got back and put the new apparel away, she would be ready for ice tea on the porch.

She was interrupted in her thoughts by Benjamin's voice, "Harold called me, he has the lady in to make meals for a couple of days and scheduled the normal cleaning. He thought we might be busy and not want to cook. We can change the menu. What do you think, Betty? Should we just do the breakfast ourselves and let her know if we will be there for lunch and or dinner?"

"Well, it's really up to JC, it's her home. I don't mind cooking but then it would also be nice to do all the things JC told me about; horseback riding, fishing, knowing the countryside and maybe helping to plan a wedding."

"That sounds good to me. Remember how nice it was to find the food in the refrigerator when we were going through the boxes and all. We could be free to come, go, and eat out if we wanted to. I'm sure Harold and John will want us over there one night too. I'll give Helen a call. While I'm at it, is there anything in particular either of you would like to eat?" JC twisted around a bit to look at Betty.

"Anything is fine with me. How does she know how much to make and who buys it?"

"The way it works, she has a credit card for groceries. John took care of any other purchases and then the bills went to Mr. Larsen, the attorney. Once I became the official owner, the bills came to me. Now, they will need to be okayed by JC." Benjamin smiled over at her.

"It's hard to believe that I really am the owner, for real, not just visiting. Thank you." Tears brightened her eyes and she blinked quickly a couple of times.

As Benjamin slowed down to make the corner into the lane, the sun shown over the mansion giving it a magical appearance.

Betty leaned forward as much as her seatbelt would allow, "It really is beautiful."

Benjamin's phone rang. He came to a stop as he took the phone from his shirt pocket.

"Hello." There was pause as he listened and glanced at his watch. "Okay. Thanks, good job." He put the phone back in his pocket, unhooked the seat belt and turned toward the ladies.

"We are going to have some guests for awhile. I know I should have run this by you earlier, JC, forgive me, but I need some peace of mind." He took a hold of her hand.

JC gave him a quizzical look, "Guests from New York? Do I know them? Give you peace of mind? I don't understand."

"Well, in about an hour, I need to pick up four men from the airport. They are coming in on my plane. Their job is to be body guards until we find out who sent you the card and if there will be anymore. We slipped up on Tim, not thinking he would do anything malicious towards you, I'm not taking changes again." He lifted her hand and kissed it. "My world would end if anything happened to you."

Removing her hand from his, "I don't like the fact that you went behind my back and did this without consulting with me. I can take care of myself; I have for all these years. I'm a trained police woman!" She opened the door, slammed it shut, and stamped her feet as she went up the steps almost tripping over a box that had her full name and a New York postmark.

CHAPTER TWENTY-FIVE

Mike Dawson printed the picture of JC from his phone. He had forgotten he had a few shots of her. Why he took one of her walking to the table was sheer luck for him. Man her figure did wonders for that blue gown. Taking one of his frames, he replaced her photo in it and sat it on his bedside table. He didn't have a lot of guests and when he did, he'd put it in the drawer.

Glancing into the full-length mirror, he thought he was looking more toned. He had been working out twice a day, not eating enough to keep that stray cat that gets into the trash happy, he should be losing weight. Picking up the frame, he traced her face with his still pudgy finger. *I wonder if she liked the flower arrangement I sent her?*

He smiled at how he had pulled off getting the flowers sent anonymously. Purchasing a bottle of cheap rotgut whiskey, he wrapped a twenty-dollar bill around it and approached the drunk who was always panhandling by the floral shop. One look at that full-unopened bottle and money and the drunk would have done just about anything.

All he had to do was give the drunk a print out from the shop of the plant he wanted sent, the exact amount of money, and the address with a sealed card that would go with the arrangement. He waited around the corner until the drunk came out with the receipt, handed over the bottle with the cash to him and then Mike went to his waiting cab. No one could trace him on this one either.

Giving the cabbie an address down town, he smiled inwardly at his cleverness. He was keeping a copy of each note he wrote at home. How many more notes would he have to send until he lost enough weight so he could deliver a gift in person?

This one wasn't what he was capable of writing, but he was afraid his style of journalism might come through and he would be found out before he was ready to make himself known.

> May this planter bloom
> And give you as much joy
> As your beauty does for me.

He sighed as the cab passed a billboard advertising one of the better restaurants. He would like some wine, a few hors d'oeuvres, some more wine to go along with a lobster smothered in butter, and the Alfredo covered noodles, their specialty cream pie and completing the meal a nightcap of Southern Comfort. He licked his lips just thinking about it. Then the image of his wonderful Janice took away the impulse to eat.

"Leave me off at the next block." He told the cabbie. He paid the fare, waiting until it moved into traffic and hailed another one to take him back to his apartment.

* * *

JC stood still looking at the box with a floral return address on it. Looking over at Benjamin, in a small voice asked, "Did you order any flowers for me?"

"No," was his terse reply. "Do you want to open it here or take it to the police station? It could be dangerous. I don't know who would have sent you this besides the person who mailed you the card. There might be some other clue or another card in it. We can also have them investigate on who sent it, how they paid for it and if they can give a description of the person."

"I agree. And, I'm sorry I snapped at you. This is all so unnerving. I'm use to country living, not shootings, houses wrecked and some creep sending me things." She wrapped her arms around him, drawing strength. Taking a deep breath, she calmly spoke, "Let's take the box in to the captain now."

Betty stood on the bottom step her arms filled with boxes. "Help me take the rest of the purchases in the mansion, I'll put them away while you two go down to the station, see what is in the box and pick up the four men."

The three quickly emptied the Explorer of the day's shopping. Benjamin picked up the box and placed it in the back seat, apprehensive of what it would hold. With all the bombings going on, one never knew. In the meantime, he would assume it was the mysterious admirer of his intended.

Leaning over he gave her a kiss. "I love you. Let's think about setting a date for the wedding."

The fear left her eyes, "I think that is a wonderful idea. Who would want to send flowers to an old married lady?"

He kissed her again, "I would, to my lady."

* * *

The captain looked at the box on his desk. "Did you notice that he used your full name, Janice Caroline Smith the same as was on your card?"

They had scanned the box and it didn't hold any explosives. "Time to open it." Wearing gloves he carefully opened the box to take out the plant and card. The technician checked for fingerprints and on the card they also checked for any traces of saliva.

"It appears all that is in here are the flowers. Are these your favorite, JC?"

"No." She said in a dejected tone.

"I have detectives in New York I've used on some cases that I want to check out the address of the flower shop. Maybe we can find out who ordered the flowers and how the payment was made. Is that okay with you captain?"

"Yes, but I want to talk with them, have their names, phone number and address. Do you think we should contact the police department there?"

Shaking his head no Benjamin replied, "Not yet. They are too busy to be involved in what could simply be a crush on someone. We are the ones who are being cautious and want to know who this unknown is. I've dealt with them in other cases of harassment and they would want more of a death threat." Moving through his phone, he produced the number of his business and also that of the detective organization, reaching for the pad of paper, wrote them down for the captain. "Do you want me to call them and leave your name and number or do you want to?"

Pulling the pad towards him, the captain looked up at him, "I want to. You trust them to not brush this off as a jealousy concern on your part?"

"Yeah. And I should tell you," he glanced at his watch, "In twenty minutes I am picking up four body guards for round the clock watch at the mansion and anywhere JC is if I'm not with her." Benjamin held up his hand to stop the captain, "I know you are capable of having this done, but with JC not on the force right now, you are already short one person. Again, I've used these men before. They are trained, licensed to carry, and proficient in martial arts. They are good looking guys who I will let on are just friends visiting here. Why not drive out later and I'll introduce them to you and you can explain how you want things handled if a problem does surface. I will also let John and Harold know who they are."

The captain came around his desk and touched Benjamin on the shoulder, "I like working with you." Then he gave JC a hug. "Well, my dear, it looks like we have our entire basis covered. We'll find out if this is a secret admirer or a dangerous man. I'll see you when I'm done with my shift and meet the four men."

As the young couple left, he made some notes and put them in a folder. This could be nothing, or she could be in danger. He would rather err on the cautious side than have JC hurt.

CHAPTER TWENTY-SIX

Benjamin pulled a few more chairs into the circle on the porch as Betty carried out a tray with a pitcher of lemonade, glasses and some sodas.

Just as Harold's old truck pulled up, the four young bodyguards came around the corner of the house along with JC who had been giving them a short tour.

Walking down the steps to the truck Benjamin opened the truck door, "Welcome and thanks for coming over. I know it's getting a little late." As Harold and John climbed the steps, another vehicle slowly came up the lane to the house. Captain Gordon kept his word about joining them.

Benjamin introduced the three men to Chet, the blond, Bob with a shaved head, Jim, with curly red hair and Juan, sporting the jet black hair of his Mexican heritage.

After everyone was seated, Benjamin spoke, "Gentlemen, these four men," he swept his hand toward the body guards, "will be escorting JC or be in her close proximity at all times. They will take turns guarding the house even though we have the alarm system in. John and Harold, I didn't want you to be alarmed with strangers here. Captain Gordon knew they were coming. As far as the community will know, the men are friends of mine from New York on vacation, just visiting." Benjamin could see the puzzled look on John and Harold's faces.

"You both may think I'm jumping to conclusions, but JC has received two pieces of mail from New York. There is no signature or return address. Both have poems declaring her beauty. We don't know if this is a nut case out there and she is in danger of being kidnapped or someone playing games." Benjamin's eyes narrowed, "Until we know who it is, we aren't taking any chances."

Old John looked over at his son, Harold, "Guess we better make sure the shot guns are clean and the buckshot close by." He slowly got up and went to JC, "Don't worry any, you will be safe. And you young men," he turned to face the body guards, "you can tackle anyone you want but if you hear me holler 'duck' hit the ground, cause those guns do scatter some."

"Now, John," Captain Gordon spoke up, "Take it easy. You watch the side roads and fields for any unusual activity or vehicles. Let the boys here keep the house covered."

Taking a sip of the lemonade, he raised the glass and remarked to Betty, "Very good."

"Thank you," Betty smiled at him.

Old John slowly sat back down, but everyone knew he meant business.

Chet, the older of the four went over and hunkered down by John and in a low voice, "Sir, later could we talk about the lay of the land here, the best way to keep the whole place covered twenty-four seven? Plus, we only carry pistols, so that shotgun might come in handy."

John looked at the young man but didn't see any signs of disrespect or playing him for a fool. "Tomorrow, you go out back of the mansion and follow that dirt road to the next place. I live there with my son since I had some surgery a while back. Otherwise, I'd be in the guest house out yonder. We'll do some talking then. Oh, and make sure you close any gates, don't want any cattle getting into the fields."

Chet nodded at John, "Tomorrow, say 7 AM, or is that too early?"

"Make it six and we can have breakfast together. You drink coffee?" John looked at him.

"Black, strong and hot." Chet smiled back at him.

John reached out his hand to shake Chet's, "See you in the morning." He liked this kid.

While John and Chet were conversing, Captain Gordon had singled out Betty. "We didn't have a chance to really talk when you came in with JC and Benjamin that day. Will you staying here all the time now?" *Gosh she is a looker.*

She leaned toward him, her light perfume pleasant but not over powering wafted faintly over him. "I'm really not sure. If we are planning a wedding, I guess I'll be here longer. Usually, I keep an eye on the law firm when Benjie is gone, but with everything that has transpired, I really wanted to be here with JC. More lemonade, captain?" *He is one handsome gentleman.*

She is such a lovely lady. "Just a half glass, then I have to get home, work tomorrow as usual." He smiled at her with his eyes and lips. "I don't suppose with everything going on around here you could slip away and we could have lunch tomorrow? It would have to be in my office since I'm expecting some calls. I can order in food."

"I think that can be arranged, but let me bring in lunch, I'm quite handy in the kitchen. Oh, and what time works for you?" She watched his eyes; they always tell you a lot about a person.

He laughed, "In my business, you never know. Shall we try for 11:30?"

"Eleven thirty it is. Any requests for lunch or do you eat anything and everything?"

"Anything, everything, and most of the times with a lot of catsup on it when I'm cooking." They both laughed.

He looked at his watch, "I hate to leave this wonderful company, but it has been a long day."

"I'll walk you to your car." Betty looped her arm through the captain's. They walked through the rest of group on the porch as if they weren't there.

When they were out of ear shot, John spoke up, "Benjamin, I think your friend and our captain took a liking to each other."

"And I think he will be back tomorrow night since his reason for coming tonight was to get acquainted with the men." Benjamin grinned. "Between you and me, I think it's great! She has been alone for many years and is like a second mom to me. I want her happy. Age has nothing to do with love."

"Yep, you're right there. Captain's been widowed for," he looked over at Harold, "About six years now?"

"Yes Dad. And I think we better call it a night too." He yawned, "We got those buildings that need painting and I suppose you want to oil your gun after breakfast."

With the men gone, Betty and JC went to their rooms. The four body guards and Benjamin went to the study after they turned on the alarms.

It was agreed one person would always be awake during the night inside the house. Crooks have been known to cut power to the house. One would always be discreetly near JC with or without Benjamin around. They all would give the same story of why they were here visiting: time away from the big city. Benjamin gave them the numbers of the police, John and Harold, the emergency service and the hospital. They would alert all of them of anything unusual or questioning and not to trust anyone.

Betty, JC and Benjamin had the bedrooms on the first floor. The men had theirs on the second floor.

Benjamin went to JC's room and saw a ray of light under the door. He tapped softly.

JC opened the door. Her long hair flowing over her shoulders gave the appearance of a younger person. She had on a pair of short summer pajamas. "I'm glad you knocked. I need a good night kiss and didn't want to interfere with the 'man' talk." She raised up her arms to hug him.

Benjamin held her tightly, leaned down and kissed her warmly. "Gosh I love you so much. Tomorrow, we set a date; announce it and plan where, how many, what type of invitations etc, etc, etc." He kissed her again very passionately.

"Hum, I agree counselor." She leaned her head against his chest, and then softly chuckled. "Maybe we should hold off. We might have to make it a double wedding. Did you see how Betty and the captain were attracted to each other like magnets?"

"I did. First we plan ours, then theirs."

"Benjamin, I need to get to bed or fall asleep standing here. I'm exhausted." JC yawned.

He kissed her. "I understand. Sweet dreams until tomorrow, my love." He gave a flourishing bow like a knight of old and backed out of the room closing the door.

Tomorrow, many plans to make. At least he could sleep knowing JC would be safe and he could sleep too. The minute his head hit the pillow, he joined the land of sound sleep.

CHAPTER TWENTY-SEVEN

"So," JC was tapping her pen against her chin as she looked over her list, "We have George and his wife. Do you want everyone at the office invited and what about Mr. and Mrs. Carson and their lovely daughter?" Her eyes were laughing as she looked at Benjamin.

"Carson family, no way, not here, but maybe for something in New York, he is prominent in business. Actually, I think we should fly George, his wife, and of course my pilots and stewardess here. I'm close to the main ones at the firm, but I don't want to fly everyone in and worry about places for them to stay etc. I want this to be a stress free day for you and me, not spent being host and hostess. Everyone else I know in New York are acquaintances, not really close friends, do you understand? We'll have a separate reception in New York after we are married and we can do the 'please the crowd bit' then. Besides, he touched her list, you know about everyone in town so the church will be standing room only as it is."

"And Honey," Benjamin took her hands in his, "I would like to have our reception at the church too, use a local catering place or we can fly in help for the food. I understand here people normally put on a meal, not have just cake and champagne for the reception. Do you think the florist here can handle everything?"

Benjamin shook his head, "I'm sorry; I'm taking over. Do you want a big wedding in New York, lots of bridesmaids, a gown from Cheree's Boutique? It's okay with me. I just want to get all the plans made so you become my wife."

Shaking her head no, "Benjamin, I don't really want a huge wedding. I want the day to be ours, not exhausted from making sure everything is done so so. I want a gown that on our anniversary I can wear again when we go out for dinner. I grew up here and want to be married in the church I've gone to all my life. Since our birth families are gone and we are really sharing our special day with wonderful friends, what if I have Betty be my matron of honor and as weird as this might sound to you, George be your best man. He is so caring and devoted to you. They are always there for you and I'm hoping Betty and I can have the same relationship as you two have."

"Are you serious?" He got up and pulled her to him. "I think that is a marvelous idea. But I thought all women wanted to be the princess of the day with a long train on their dress and twelve bridesmaids walking down the aisle."

JC leaned back and looked at him, "I don't want to be a princess for a day, I want to be a wife for the rest of our lives. Remember the shop next to Ms Rose, well, I did see the dress I would like to get. The House of Cheree's is for New York."

"The date," he picked up the calendar, "Do you think we can get it together for a month from this Saturday?"

"Let's call the Reverend Haroldson and see if the church is available. I know he always likes to do a counseling session with couples too." She giggled, "Do you really think that will be necessary at our age, but then again, neither one of us have been married before."

"Hey you two," Betty stepped into the room carrying a picnic basket. "The captain and I are having lunch at his office. Helen is almost ready for the rest of you. I have never seen someone so happy to have the young men to cook for."

"Wait a minute, Betty. Benjamin and I have tentatively set our date if it's okay with the pastor and," JC walked over to Betty and touched her arm, "I would like you to be my matron of honor."

Betty set the basket down and hugged her tightly looking over at a smiling Benjamin. "You want me, not your young friends?"

"We want family,"

"Yes, I'd be honored." She got teary eyed. "Very honored. And who will be the best man?"

"George if he will."Benjamin replied, "I know most people wouldn't have their chauffeur, but he is always there for me as he was mom and dad. I trust him and he is like family to me."

Betty clapped her hands together, "This is so great! Let me know what the pastor says and then we have got some real planning to do, when I return." She glanced at her watch, "I need to go, I promised Gordon I'd be there at 11:30."

Laughing JC remarked, "I don't think he would have you arrested if you were a minute late."

The young couple watched as Jim opened the Jeep door for her then went around to the driver's side. Betty had never had to learn to drive a vehicle living in the city.

Chet came around the corner as the Jeep went down the lane. He took the steps two at a time and joined the couple on the porch.

"I had a very interesting morning with John and Harold. As far as they are concerned, you are their little girl and woe to anyone that wants to hurt a hair on your head." He grinned at her then turned serious. "What is the disturbing episode that happened recently concerning you because they gave off the feeling to me that they are partly responsible?"

Benjamin and JC exchanged glances. JC spoke up, "Harold's son Tim had a crush on me. He also has a drinking problem. While I was in New York, he broke into my house and trashed it. None of us thought he would have ever done anything like that. The worst thing was the note written in lipstick on the bathroom wall, 'if I can't have you, no one will'. It was rather upsetting to me." Tears formed in her eyes.

Benjamin took her hand in his, "You're safe and he is getting the help he needs." The two then related the whole situation to Chet.

"That explains everything. Well, I thoroughly enjoyed my visit with them and have the lay of the land in my mind. John also showed me his guns he is so proud of and the faithful shotgun. He feels part of the team and has agreed to wait on our communication before taking any action. I really don't want to worry about a shotgun going off while we are doing our job." He smiled.

The sound of a triangle bell got their attention. JC laughed, "Helen is announcing dinner, or lunch however you want to call it is ready. That is always used for family; you can hear it outside too."

Chet got up immediately, "I'm ready, and breakfast was a long time ago." He wasted no time leading the way through the house to the kitchen.

"I told Helen we would take our meals in the kitchen instead of the dining room. I don't want to make any more work for her. Is that alright with you?" JC spoke low as they followed Chet.

"Of course. Speaking of that, do you need more help here when George and his wife get here?"

"She has a daughter who will come in to assist if or when she needs it and we will use the dining room then. After lunch, we need to call pastor." Tilting her head up, she received the kiss she wanted.

* * *

"I don't have an opening for the church until the first weekend in October. Will that be alright?" Pastor Haroldson tapped his appointment book with his pen and looked over his glasses at them.

JC answered for them both, "That makes it six weeks from tomorrow. Perfect. We need to get the license, invitations, flowers and everything. Oh, and we would like to have the reception here too, we were thinking having a 4:00 wedding with the dinner to follow."

"Are you having it catered or did you want the ladies aid to do it."

Benjamin leaned forward, "We thought of bringing in a catering service because they will clean up afterwards, if that is okay with you. It will be a sit down one. If we had sandwiches and cake it might be different."

"Actually, our ladies do put on many dinners and we have some college aged ones that can help. They would do it as a fundraiser. It depends on how fancy you want it." Pastor responded.

Benjamin shared a look with JC. "It's up to you, honey."

"Well, they are fabulous cooks, everything would be nice. We just need to do the decorations and we can pay the kids to remove them. I don't want a lot, but to keep it simple."

"The ladies aid society it is then." Benjamin smiled.

The three spent the next hour discussing marriage and the responsibilities of each one. It was informative and reinforced to them both that this was what they wanted in a marriage.

Their next stop was to see Alice who was the president of the ladies aid society to make all the arrangements for the reception.

Later as they sat in the Explorer, JC put a small 'x' behind the word pastor and reception. "Now, I think we should order the invitations, thank you notes, and napkins. If we have time, perhaps we should check out the floral shop and..." she paused looking over at him, "What about a photographer?"

"By all means. We should have a photo taken and sent to the paper in New York to Mike Dawson announcing our engagement. He is in charge of that department. Then this photographer can do the wedding pictures. Do you have one here to use or should I get one?" Benjamin started the vehicle.

"Let's do the local one. They do all the graduations and weddings around here." She smiled.

"Okay, then give me the directions to the printer, if enough time, the photographers. Oh, we should make that announcement picture a formal one. Do you want to wear the gown you brought with or purchase a new one?" Benjamin pulled out into the street.

"I don't know, I'll see what Betty thinks, okay."

"Okay." *Six weeks. He wished it was tomorrow.*

CHAPTER TWENTY-EIGHT

Mike picked up the stack of mail from his inbox and sorted through them flipping some into the wastebasket when he stopped with his hand in midair. The return address was Benjamin Murphy from Freedomville. His heart started to race, and sweat formed on his forehead. *Did the prominent attorney figure out he was the one who sent the card and flowers to beautiful Janice Caroline?*

Pulling his monogrammed white handkerchief from his pocket he wiped the sweat off his forehead. Quickly he looked around; everyone was busy at their desks and not paying any attention to him. He took a deep breath and a swig from the water bottle, willing himself to calm down. The facts were he was careful that no one saw him mail the card and the drunk he had order the flowers wouldn't be able to identify him either he was so inebriated. He took a deep breath willing himself to relax.

He slid the letter opener across the envelope. Removing the card he was surprised to see a photo of his Janice Caroline with that Murphy's arm around her. Ah, she was so beautiful. With his finger he lightly touched her face mentally putting his image where Benjamin was. Placing the picture on his desk, he picked up the letter.

Dear Mr. Dawson,

As the social editor, we are sending you our engagement announcement. I will let you know when a reception is to be held in New York.

Yours truly,
Benjamin Murphy

'Janice Smith, police officer and Benjamin Murphy, President of the Murphy Law Firm are pleased to announce their engagement. An October wedding will be held in Miss Smith's hometown of Freedomville. A reception will be held in New York following their honeymoon. After their marriage they will reside both in Freedomville and in New York.'

The sheet of paper shook in Mike's hand. He was frustrated and angry. Twice a day for weeks now he had been working out diligently, starving himself so he prove to her what a man he was and now, in what, six weeks, his beloved was going to marry that rich attorney who had women falling all over themselves to get his attention! It wasn't fair! Well... he ran his hand through his hair, he had to think of something, he couldn't let this farce of a marriage happen. But what? Anyone could see that Murphy was just toying with her, look at all those rich babes available: money begets money and she was a poor country girl who probably wouldn't allow him in her bed without a wedding ring on her finger. The ink would probably just be dry on the marriage certificate and he would be looking for a new interest that's what all those rich cats did. He knew, he wrote up all those engagements, marriages and divorces. He saw them sneaking out on their wives. Oh, he could write a book about it.

Making a copy of their picture, he placed it in his briefcase, and then forwarded the announcement and picture to the printing department along with his regular column.

Later that evening after his workout and shower, he removed the couple's picture from his briefcase. Sitting down at his desk, he carefully cut JC from the picture and put Benjamin's up on his dartboard. Then he trimmed his Janice Caroline's picture even more so it didn't show Benjamin's arm around her waist and put it in his billfold.

Leaving just the bed side lamp on, he propped his pillows up against his headboard on his bed and taking her photo from the bedside table, laid down remembering what it felt like to hold her in his arms for that short time on the dance floor.

Six weeks. He had six short weeks to decide what to do. He could go there, proclaim his love to her or... wait until after the honeymoon and arrange an accident for Murphy. Then again, he could be patient until Murphy had his fling with her and started meeting with say, oh that Carson girl and he, Mr. Dawson could go to Janice Caroline's rescue, let her cry on his now, more muscular shoulder.

He smiled to himself; he could make that breakup happen by writing something in his column that really wasn't true. Reporters didn't follow any of the rules anymore. A word here, a word there can give off a connotation of something that appears true and isn't. Sometimes it scared him how he came up with so many interesting ideas.

Sitting up, he put her photo back on the table. Going to the kitchen, he fixed himself one of those protein drinks with a muscled man on the side, and then it was time for another workout while he planned his next step.

* * *

The UPS truck came to a stop in front of the mansion. Juan met the driver as he brought the large box up the steps of the porch.

Juan took a look at the return address. "Wait one moment before I sign for this." He went inside and wrapped on the doorframe of the open door of the office. "Benjamin, another box from New York."

The two men went back to the porch and when Benjamin saw the return address from The House of Cheree, he let out a sigh of relief, and quickly signed for it, thanking the driver for waiting.

"Thanks Juan, but this," he tapped the box, "This is a dress I ordered for JC, to replace the one that she wore the night I was shot."

Juan smiled; he knew how ladies like nice clothes. He saluted Benjamin and went outside.

CHAPTER TWENTY-NINE

The cracking fire sent off flickers of light across the room giving a cozy atmosphere as the couple relaxed.

"I can't believe everything we've accomplished in these last six weeks." JC snuggled against Benjamin's shoulder.

Benjamin chuckled, "We've both been busy." He held out his fingers as he listed each item. "All the arrangements for our wedding and honeymoon are taken care of. You have your city council, the zoning board and Mr. Larsen to thank for getting all the legalities out of the way for the foundation. In the city we would still be on the waiting list."

"It was amazing how quickly my home was bulldozed down and the NEW LIFE CENTER building begun." JC giggled, "And to think that tomorrow my name will be part of the 'Murphy Foundation'.

"Hey you two lovebirds, I made some tea for three." Betty placed the tray on the table in front of them. "The third cup is for me. George and Claire are in the kitchen playing MONOPOLY with the boys." Just as she was to pour the tea, Jim who was on duty for the evening interrupted them.

"Boss, I don't feel too good. My stomach is really bothering me. I need to lay down awhile. I'll get one of the other guys to take my place." He held his hand by his side.

JC and Benjamin went to him, "I can give the doc a call or take you in." JC placed her hand on his arm.

"I don't know what it is; maybe I ate something that isn't setting just right. If I can just rest for awhile, it will probably pass."

"If you don't feel better in an hour, we are taking you into the Urgent Care. In the meantime, can we get you some tea or water?" JC didn't like his ashen complexion, and these men were tough Navy Seals, not wimps that would lie down from a bit of indigestion.

Jim shook his head no. He slowly moved in the direction of the kitchen.

"Wait, Jim. Was everything quiet out there?" Benjamin asked.

"Yes, sir."

"Just go rest, you don't need to notify any of the men, I think we will be okay. I'll turn on the alarm system when I go to bed. Remember, if you feel worse, light headed anything, call out." Benjamin patted Jim's shoulder.

The three watched as Jim slowly made his way up the stairs.

"Do you think it is wise not to have someone on duty?" Betty questioned Benjamin.

"There hasn't been any other mail, *no* phone calls, *no* mysterious strangers around so I think we will be okay. Besides, with everyone in the house, who would want to try anything? Now, I would like some of that tea." He held up his cup.

They all took a seat and Betty poured the tea. "Are you both ready for tomorrow?"

"Yes," they both replied in unison, smiles on their faces as they exchanged loving glances.

Taking a sip of her tea, Betty commented, "I'm surprised you both aren't in a dizzy, since tomorrow is the big day."

Leaning forward JC placed her hand on Betty's knee, "Because of all your organization, everything has gone smoothly. Tomorrow I'm marrying the most wonderful man in the world, the love of my life." She smiled at Benjamin, "And you Betty have become a mother in my life. Thank you for being you."

Betty embraced the young woman and Benjamin teared up with emotion… he would once again have a family; he had felt so alone after his parents died.

Wiping their eyes, the three happy people settled back in their chairs.

Betty questioned, "Are you two going to see each other tomorrow or wait until the ceremony, you know the traditional thing?"

"I don't believe in the bad luck of not seeing each other before the wedding. Betty, you and I will ride with John, and I think Chet will be driving. Chet wants to make sure John leaves 'ole Betsy' his shot gun at home."

They chuckled knowing how protective John was about them all.

JC continued, "George, Claire, Benjamin and Juan will travel together. Jim is supposed to stay here and Bob will circulate around the church just in case anyone weird shows up uninvited."

"Are you dressing here or at the church? I think at the church would eliminate messing up your dress." Betty picked up the teapot to refresh the cups with more tea.

"I agree. Are you dressing there too?" JC asked.

"Oh no. I'll be busy zipping you up." They all laughed.

"Did I tell you the ladies at the church would make sure the flowers were in place in the church when they are delivered tomorrow morning?" JC smiled, "I've been so lucky to have everyone be so helpful."

Benjamin stood up, "I'm going to go check on Jim, glance over my email and then call it a night." He took JC in his arms kissing her warmly. "You get some rest too; tomorrow will be a long and busy day."

"Yes Sir." She saluted him.

JC stayed there by herself thinking about her past and the wonderful future ahead of her until only a few embers were left burning. She shut off the lights and went to her room, never noticing that the window was still open.

* * *

Mike couldn't believe his good luck as he stayed in the shadow of the hedges that lined the driveway where he wasn't noticed. As he moved closer, he saw the man that had been patrolling the perimeter of the house and yard sit down on the top step and hold his abdomen. It wasn't long and he moved over and threw up in the bushes. Then he entered the house by the front door.

Not seeing any motion sensor lights or anyone else, Mike hurried toward the mansion. He could hear voices, staying close to the building he carefully angled near the open window. He recognized his wonderful Janice Caroline's voice. He glanced around looking for something to stand on to peek into the room. A wheel barrel was left to one side where someone had been working on the yard. Quietly he maneuvered it to the side of the window and carefully stepped into it so he could just barely look into the bottom part of the window.

His blood pressure soared as he saw his Janice with her head against that lawyer. That should be him. Well, it would be soon, he had to work quickly since she was to marry tomorrow. He had to save her from future heartache when the prestigious Mr. Murphy was bound to get tired of her like all rich men did.

He listened to the whole conversation. Ah, he could remove her from the car tomorrow. It sounded like it would be that small lady and some old man with her. Oh yah, and a driver. He patted his pocket that held the gun he paid plenty for on the black market. He smiled at how clever he was no papers to trace him to the gun. Everyone at work thought he was visiting his mother. Mom, ha, that old bag had been dead for ten years, but he still owned the house. That's where he was taking his lovely Janice Caroline. He smiled as he thought of all his clever plans, why he even had the refrigerator stocked with food. Her new clothes he had picked out for her were hanging in the closet.

Everyone was leaving the room except his beloved Janice Caroline; she stayed quietly watching the fire until there was just a few coals left then she shut off the light and left the room. Soon he saw a light from another window and moved the wheelbarrow over to it. Yes, it was her bedroom. The door opened from what he assumed was the bathroom, she came out ready for bed wearing pajamas, and the light went off.

What to do now? He felt nervous. Touching the bottle of chloroform in his pocket he wondered, should he sneak through the living room window and take her or wait until tomorrow? His attention was diverted by seeing Murphy helping that guy that threw up out to the Jeep in the front. No one followed them, and he didn't see anyone else moving around in the house.

Mike crouched tight against the house and watched until the taillights could no longer be seen. Putting on rubber gloves he slowly walked around the corner and cautiously up the steps surprised to find the door left open. He tried the screen door and there was no sound as he pulled it just wide enough to get in.

The entry way and the surrounding area was dimly lit. Waiting a minute to get his eyes adjusted to the light, he looked around seeing what he thought was the living room. He moved slowly, not wanting to trip or bump into any furniture. To the right looked like a den or office and to the left, he wasn't sure, there were a lot of plants in there. The next room had the fireplace. Ah, then the room his love was in. That door was closed. How he hoped those hinges on the door were as well oiled as the others and not locked. Looking around, seeing no one, he gently turned the doorknob hoping she was asleep. He didn't want her screaming and waking everyone up.

His heart was beating so hard he was afraid she might hear it. *Slow down, deep breath.* Sweat beaded on his forehead.

The faint moonlight coming through the window outlined the furniture in the room. There she was, curled up in that big bed like the one he had waiting for her. She had one arm out of the covers.

Putting on a mask so he wouldn't breathe in the fumes, he retrieved the bottle and a monogrammed handkerchief from his pocket. He quietly opened the bottle and poured liquid on the folded cloth drenching it. Sliding the bottle back in his jacket, he approached the bed firmly holding the wet fabric tightly over her face. She struggled briefly and was still.

Removing his mask he pulled the covers back, and picked her up. How light she felt, all those workouts gave him the muscles to do this. He couldn't wait to see how impressed she would be from all his exercising and diet. Um, could he carry her all the way down the whole lane to where he was parked? The wheel barrel, he would use that. Grabbing the blanket, he would place that in the barrel so it would be soft for her.

Retracing his steps, he had just left her room when he felt something pushed against his back that felt like a gun and another man wearing black materialized in front of him.

"Don't move a muscle." The male voice belonged to whoever held the gun.

The bald man in front of him reached for JC.

"No! She's mine!" The screaming voice startled him and then he realized it was his voice.

"Give her to me, careful now." The bald man held out his arms and took a step closer.

Mike's eyes were darting all over. He had to get away. This couldn't be happening. They wouldn't shoot him while he was holding his precious Janice Caroline.

"Calm down. You don't want to hurt JC." The bald man was talking real low and in a monotone.

"Her name is Janice Caroline. Don't call her JC. She is a lady. Now get out of my way, she's mine." Mike's voice was low and menacing.

The bright ceiling lights came on making Mike blink his eyes.

"Why, I do believe it's Mr. Dawson. I think you are disturbing Janice in her sleep. Give her to Bob and let me get you a drink. If I remember correctly, you like a good brandy." Betty slowly inched toward Mike.

Mike shook his head, he was feeling overwhelmed. His chest was pounding trying to get out. This wasn't like he planned it. He was feeling rather ill right now and he didn't want to drop his Janice Caroline. He nodded at Baldy who carefully gathered his Janice up and took her back to her bed.

He could still feel the gun at his back, but the pain was in his shoulder. Sweat was pouring down his face as he slowly drawled out, "I... don't... feel good," collapsing on the hard wood floor.

* * *

Flashing lights broke the dark of night at the two police cars sped up the lane breaking to a fast stop scattering gravel. The first one in the door was the Captain Gordon. He looked at the man on the floor then went to Betty. "Are you alright?"

She nodded. "Thank God for the silent alarm. He tried to kidnap our JC. From the smell of it he used chloroform. I think we should take her into the hospital and you can take him to jail. Watch him; it's Mike Dawson, a reporter, I think he is a psycho."

"I'll call the ambulance." The captain patted her shoulder.

"I got it Captain, they are on the way. I think he should go too. Heart is acting up; he might be having a coronary or some type of medical problem."

"Okay, better cuff him anyway, don't know if he is on some drug or not and check for an ID. I saw a car down the side road, check that out, and see who it's registered to." He turned and went to Betty who was wiping JC's face with a wet wash cloth. JC was still out cold, he could see the worry in Betty's face.

It was a relief to hear the ambulance pull up.

Betty looked up at Gordon, "Can they wait long enough for me to put some clothes on? I need to go with her."

"I'll take you. Go change." *She looked strong yet so feminine in her floor length nightgown with just her bare feet showing.*

"Will you call the hospital and page Benjamin that JC is on her way? He took Jim in about two hours ago; we think he was having an appendicitis attack. I'm sure that is why he didn't wake up one of the other men to watch the house." The words tumbled out of her. "I'll be just a minute." She stopped for a moment watching as the EMT's took both JC and Mike Dawson to the ambulance. Then it hit her why he looked so different, he must have lost close to a hundred pounds and was looking trim.

CHAPTER THIRTY

Slowly JC felt herself coming out of the foggy tunnel. Something was on her face. She raised her arm to brush it and heard her name.

"Hold still JC, you're alright." She heard a male voice and a hand on hers. JC's eyelids fluttered and she tried to focus. *Where was she?*

"I'm Dr. Allen. You are in the Emergency Room getting a little bit of oxygen and an IV. Someone drugged you and we are clearing it from your system."

JC lay still and let her eyes stop on the face. *Oh yes, Dr. Allen, the one who caught Benjamin and her kissing in the stairway.*

The door burst open and Benjamin was by her side.

"You can't barge in here like this! I'll call security." The nurse reached for the phone.

"He is with security."

The nurse stopped. "Oh, Captain Gordon, I didn't know you were here. As long as he is with you, I guess it is alright."

"Benjamin, why am I here? What happened?" JC held tight to his hand.

"Honey, it seems that Mike Dawson, the reporter who danced with you that brief time tried to kidnap you. He is also the one who sent the flowers and the card. I'll see he sits in the psyche ward or jail for a long time." He leaned down and kissed her on the forehead.

"Benjamin, could you step out in the hallway for a minute?" Captain Gordon motioned with his head.

"I'll be right back, honey." Benjamin squeezed her hand gently.

Once in the hallway, the Captain lowered his voice, "Mike Dawson had a coronary in the ambulance and was DOA. The only place he is going to is the family plot. In his wallet, he had JC's picture and two poems or verses. We checked out his rental car and he had some suitcases in there. The home address he gave for the rental info wasn't his New York apartment address. We are going to be checking that out."

"This is my entire fault. I should have woke up one of the men, and locked the door. I guess I was worried about Jim and getting him to the hospital. He is in surgery right now by the way. When we didn't receive any more cards or flowers, I really thought she would be safe since we are getting married," he looked at his watch, "today if she is feels up to it."

Betty and Chet came around the corner with a cup of coffee. "Is she alright?"

The doctor answered the question as he came out the door. "Yes, we have stopped the oxygen and as soon as the IV is done she can go home. She will have a bit of a headache, but she is fine. I don't see any complications of any kind."

The four of them entered her room to find her sitting up, her face still a little redder than normal from the effects of the chloroform. She raised her arms looking at Benjamin, who quickly went to her, holding her tightly.

Betty came around the side of the bed and gave her a hug.

The captain finished talking on the phone, clicked off then joined them.

"Tell me what happened. I feel like I'm Alice in Wonderland going down the hole." JC looked at everyone wanting a clear answer.

Each one told her what they knew with the Captain adding from his last phone call. "The officer that checked out Dawson's apartment, found your pictures and a journal in which he describes his one sided infatuation with you. Evidently he has been exercising and dieting to an extreme in order to woe you from Benjamin here, who in his estimation, Dawson felt wasn't worthy of you. He went too far with his fitness regime that he damaged his heart. He won't be troubling you anymore."

JC looked at him, "Why?"

The captain said softly, "He had a massive heart attack. Along with his extreme dieting he was taking too many of those energy drinks, it was all too much for his heart."

She shook her head in amazement, "I only spent a few seconds of a dance with him. How could that have had that effect on him?"

The nurse taking her pulse answered, "Because he was a mentally sick man. It wasn't your fault." She then removed the IV from JC's arm. "If you sign this release, you are free to go home." She handed her the clipboard.

JC signed the form and handing it back. She looked down at herself, "At least I don't have to get dressed, I'm still in my pajamas."

* * *

The sun was peeking over the horizon as all those awake sat at the kitchen having coffee and tea.

"Do you want me to cancel the wedding for today? We can always have the pastor marry us in his study or here later if you don't feel up to it." Benjamin was concerned because JC still looked rather pale.

"No way! I'm not letting that Mike person spoil our day. I want to be your wife I love you so! Give me a couple hours to get some beauty sleep. The wedding isn't until four, we can leave here at three, it is going to be our day." She stood up and they embraced warmly.

"Okay then, scoot and get some rest. What time to you want us to wake you?"

"If I'm not up by noon, wake me. I feel tired but excited too, does that make any sense?"

Everyone at the table laughed. "Perfect sense, my dear, you're a bride to be." Betty put her arm through JC's and walked with her to the bedroom. "Do you want me to stay here while you sleep or will you be okay?"

"I'll be okay, you go rest too. You were up all night and need some sleep. I can't have my maid of honor stand up next to me with dark circles under her eyes." JC hugged Betty holding tightly on to her. "I'm so glad to have you in my life and that you were here for me and Benjamin."

"That's what moms are for, to be here."

* * *

They arrived at the church around 2:30, which gave them time to check the floral arrangements, the ladies catering the meal and to make arrangements for any leftover food. The flowers would go to some of the elderly of the congregation that couldn't make it to the wedding. Pastor would deliver those.

A box to hold the wedding cards was a replica of The New Life Building which was on it's own table by the door the guests would use to enter the dining area. Benjamin and JC had requested on their wedding invitations that donations to the New Life Building foundation or to a charity of their own instead of gifts.

There were two floral arrangements besides the bouquets for JC and Betty in the room where they would change clothes. JC wanted them for later.

Now it was time to get dressed. JC had chosen a sleeveless white gown with simple flowing lines that was street length. A matching mid-arm length jacket could go with it or a very sheer lacy shawl if it was cool. Her flowers were an arrangement of autumn colors. She wore her long blond hair down wearing a small hat with a veil that came down just covering her eyes. Her only jewelry was the pearl necklace and earrings that had been her mothers. Betty gave her a blue garter to slide on her leg and a penny to put in her shoe. Betty said she didn't know why but it was tradition. They giggled about that.

There was a knock on the door. Old John was standing there with a grin that covered his whole face. He was so happy to be walking JC down the aisle.

"Ladies, the organ is playing our song." John had on his Sunday suit, and his shoes were shined so much they almost sparkled.

The three stood at the back of the crowded church and watched as Pastor Haroldson took his place and then nodded to Benjamin and George to take their places. Seeing John and the ladies, he then motioned to the organist, who changed into the music they had requested to walk up the aisle.

Betty walked slowly to the front and stood to one side.

JC with her arm through John's, kept her eyes on Benjamin as they slowly made their way to stop in front of the pastor.

"Who gives this woman to wed?"

Harold stood up and so did the whole congregation. John turned sideways and raised his hand and they all said, "We do!"

With moist eyes, John placed JC's hand in Benjamin's, "Take care son, and love our girl with all your heart," he stepped back and sat down next to his son pulling out that big old blue handkerchief and blew his nose.

Pastor Haroldson opened up his bible and smiling out at the congregation reminisced, "Many years ago, my father married Janice Caroline's parents in this same church. It is a privilege for me to marry their daughter to Benjamin, the grandson of a wonderful man, Willard Murphy, a much loved member of our congregation."

The Pastor shared a few hilarious childhood times that Janice had with her grandparents and the Murphy family. Then he gave the marriage instructions and had them say their vows.

"With the power invested in me by the church and state, I now pronounce you husband and wife. What God has joined together let no man put asunder. You may kiss your bride."

And Benjamin did causing many smiles and clapping from those in attendance.

At the reception when everyone was seated and the food was being served, Old John slowly stood up and took the microphone, tapping it making sure it was on.

"I'm not good at this but I'm standing in for JC's folks, and Willard. JC has been like a daughter to me and as I've gotten to know Benjamin here," he paused and put his hand on Benjamin's shoulder, "I'd say he is a chip off his granddad's block. I've grown very fond of him."

There was cheering and clapping. John held up his hand, "Now, the kids didn't plan this, but my boy and I have made arrangements at the country club for a dance band so you can work off the calories from this fabulous dinner the ladies have provided. I just want you to know that after the first dance with her husband, I get dibs on the second turn around the floor." John sat down to laughter and applause. He was much loved by them all.

After the reception, Benjamin and JC took the two bouquets she has specially ordered to the cemetery. They placed one by the headstone of her parents and grandparents, the other by Benjamin's grandparents. As the couple stood there hand and hand, JC spoke, "Mom, Dad, grandma and grandpa and Elizabeth and Willard, Benjamin and I were married today and these flowers are from our wedding. I'm happy."

Benjamin spoke, "I didn't know any of you, but rest assured I love Janice Caroline Smith Murphy with all my heart."

Who knows where the spirit of our loved ones are but in the young married couple's mind, they believe the family heard them and appreciated the visit and the flowers.

* * *

At the dance, the captain came up to JC for a whirl around the floor. "I wanted you to know that Chet has filled out an application for your position and I wouldn't be surprised if Jim doesn't apply too. They both have an excellent record in the service as Navy Seals and had some training in police work. I think a short six weeks will qualify them. I think Jim may go into our small detective department. Thanks for suggesting them."

Lowering his voice, "Does Benjamin really need Betty as his consultant? Could she move here?" His face got red, as he stammered, "I, I am rather fond of her."

JC had all she could do not to laugh out loud. "I think Benjamin will always think of her as his mom and come to her as I will for motherly advice." Then she got a mischievous grin on her face, "You go for it, she is a lovely lady and no doubt will have no problem relocating to our fair town of Freedomville. You have my blessings and I'm sure Benjamin's."

With the magic hour of midnight, Benjamin and JC slipped away from the happy dancing crowd to the waiting airplane and off to their secret honeymoon and a new life as, Mr. and Mrs. Benjamin Murphy.

The End

EPILOGUE

ONE YEAR LATER

JC and Benjamin are the proud parents of Margaret Ann who was born on their first year anniversary. She was named after both her grandmothers.

The NEW LIFE BUILDING was completed and the programs over seen by the Murphy Foundation of which JC is the president assisted by Betty.

This new chemical and mental rehabilitation organization provided new direction of life patterns for those in need. Counseling, classes in job skills, nutrition training and money management were mandatory.

One stipulation to being enrolled in the program was no illegal drugs or alcohol consumption would be tolerated while enrolled in the program.

Those in the program were to keep their room's clean, assist with the cooking and cleaning up when not in class. The premise being idle hands get depressed, busy people have a reason to learn, change, and feel good about themselves.

The chapel was available at all times for meditation. For those who wished to attend Sunday services, they were conducted by rotating ministers from the surrounding communities.

This new venture also provided employment for the community and allowed others to volunteer in their area of knowledge.

Betty and Gordon were engaged with a small spring wedding in the planning. Gordon was also promoted to sheriff.

Oh John remained living with his son, but was a frequent visitor to the mansion. He also made a cradle for Margaret Ann, who he considers his great granddaughter.

Harold became mayor of Freedomville and was very happy when his son Tim beat his alcohol addiction, and was one of the first to complete the classes at The NEW LIFE BUILDING.

Benjamin still commuted to the Big Apple to conduct his law firm business and JC would accompany him. They also turned one of the bedrooms at the condo into a nursery.

Accompanying them on the trips was a young woman widowed when her husband was killed in action. She became a full time nanny for Margaret Ann. The nanny was also encouraged by the Murphy family to take online courses to further her education.

Chet and Jim were hired on full time as police officers.

Life was good in Freedomville, USA.

ABOUT THE AUTHOR

Donna Bryan was born and raised in La Crosse, Wisconsin, a town full of history with the mighty Mississippi River flowing by separating it from Minnesota. The city spreads out into farmland with Granddad Bluff watching over it. Even Mark Twain in *Life on the Mississippi* mentioned Granddad Bluff, from the top where one can see three states.

Donna has also lived in Minnesota and Missouri with her family. Throughout these moves, she has always enjoyed writing articles, worship services, children's stories, and programs.

The Mansion is Donna's second published book. Her first book was *Truck Drivin' Man: Warrior of the Road*. She hopes you enjoy reading her books as much as she did writing them.

More about Donna and her latest writing projects can be found at: www.DonnaMBryan.com.

DONNA M. BRYAN

Printed in Great Britain
by Amazon